KickAss Plays
for Women

FOUR SHORT PLAYS

by

Jane Shepard

FOUNDED 1830

NEW YORK HOLLYWOOD LONDON TORONTO

SAMUELFRENCH.COM

PLAY

ISBN 978-0-573-66343-7   Printed in U.S.A.   #12987

IMPORTANT BILLING AND CREDIT
REQUIREMENTS

WELCOME

From the Playwright

Life is not free of pain and neither are these plays. But it's also full of beauty, and absurdity, and stuff that makes you laugh hard enough to blow milk out your nose. And it's full of blessings, the divine & the human, and sometimes they're the same. In the moments when you just can't jump the hurdle, it is astonishing that circumstance (or one's own preposterousness) will nudge us into somebody's path. Someone who sees you over that hurdle, or just sees you. And it makes all the difference. That is the alchemy of which human beings are capable. To take the frozen coal of another's despair and transform it, through connection, to the gold of moving forward.

Whether you're man or woman, actor, director or reader, you are welcome to these plays. Look for a passage where you find a little scrap of your own truth and take it with you. May it steady your faith in the whole gut-wrenching, hair-raising, spit-flying, laugh-out-loud, deep dance of being alive. The wounds and the healing are what add up to make you deep and wide and wiggly. The full scope of personhood. It's a kickass thing.

– Jane Shepard

CONTENTS

THE PLAYWRIGHT WISHES TO THANK

To my Kickass Collaborators who helped and inspired this collection:, Vanessa Shealy, who proofed just 'cause she's nice; website guru Benjamin Winn; and Donna LaStella for software guidance and sharing her beautiful family.

Publishing Mentors: Betsy Buck, Brus Westby, Kent Shepard, Bill & Marnie Winn, and my father, Paul Shepard.

Creative Mentors: Lanford Wilson, Marsha Norman, and Michael Warren Powell. Playwright Arlene Hutton and Eleanor Speert at the Drama Bookshop, NY for their professional wisdom. And to the Off-Off-Broadway companies everywhere who give new writers hope & productions. Especially Circle Rep and One Dream Theatre (R.I.P.), as well as Circle East, and Stephen Sunderlin at Vital Theatre Company.

Thank you to the immensely inspiring actors & directors who worked on these and other productions of the plays, from whom I learn so much, and who make the plays worth writing:

Actors Kate Bennis, Colleen Davenport, Pamela Dunlap, Kit Flanagan, Donna Jean Fogel, Katt Lissard, Joan Rater, Molly Powell, Vanessa Shealy, George Sheffey, and Jessica Weglein.

Directors Michele Coleman, Julie Hamberg, Gregor Paslawsky, Michael Warren Powell, and Andrea "Spook" Testani.

To Marnie & Bill Winn at PuppetArtists for their amazing designs on THE LAST NICKEL (PuppetArtists.com.) And to Melba, 'cause she always believes.

PHOTO CREDITS

Cover Photo: Molly Powell appearing in the film version of NINE. *Photo: Susan Michie.*

Title Page NINE: Donna Jean Fogel and Kit Flanagan in the Circle Rep Lab production, directed by Michele Coleman. *Photo: Jane Shepard.*

Title Page COMMENCING: Kate Bennis and Colleen Davenport. *Photo: Jane Shepard.*

Title Page FRIENDS OF THE DECEASED: Vanessa Shealy and Pamela Dunlap appearing in Vital Theatre Company's production, directed by Andrea "Spook" Testani. *Photo: Vital Theatre.*

Title Page THE LAST NICKEL: Jane Shepard and Kate Bennis, appearing in Laine Valentino's production at One Dream, directed by Julie Hamberg. *Photo: Julie Hamberg.*

NINE

Donna Jean Fogel and Kit Flanagan at the Circle Rep Lab

SETTING

A locked room, a cell or basement.

TIME

40 minutes, blackout between first & second parts.

ROLES

1 & 2, the women being held there.

PART I

(A LOCKED ROOM, could be a cell, probably a basement.

***AT RISE:** TWO WOMEN each chained by the neck to opposite walls. 2 is slumped, unmoving & withdrawn. 1 watches HER, silent for a time.)*

1. Hurt?

(Silence.)

2. Hm?

1. Are you hurt?

2. No.

1. They didn't hurt you?

2. No.

1. I didn't think so.

(SHE waits.)

Can you sit up?

2. Yes.

1. Come on then.

2. No. I'm very tired.

1. Tired from the day?

2. Huh?

1. Tired from the day?

2. I don't want to talk now.

1. Just tell me this.

(2 doesn't move or reply.)

Just tell me what you're tired from.

2. No.

1. Are you tired from working?

(Silence.)

Answer me.

(Silence.)

Please.

(Silence.)

Hey.

2. Please let me rest.

1. You just said you were tired, and so, is it tired from rest or tired from work or just worn out from your day? One gets weary in a number of ways.

*(**2** rolls closer to the wall.)*

Because if it's weariness from just the day –

2. From work, from work, I'm tired from work. Now just… let it go.

1. Ah, she's tired from work! She worked too hard. She's worn out. Okay, very good, I see that. That's fair enough. Can I see your face?

2. Shuttup now.

1. Okay, fair enough, you're tired, you've worn yourself out, it's been a long day, I've had 'em myself, I just need to see your hand.

(Nothing)

Come on, your hand. Just one. Your hand. One. Then you can rest. After I see your hand.

*(**2** lifts a hand, drops it.)*

Uh! No, I didn't see that, I'm slow on the uptake, so show it again, hold it up here in the light. Let's go!

*(**2** thrusts hand up again.)*

Wiggle….

*(**2** wiggles fingers.)*

1. Bend.

(Bends fingers.)

Good.

(Drops hand.)

Other hand.

2. Fuck you.

1. Fine, but with your other hand.

(Nothing.)

Don't make me sing.

(No reply. 1 SINGS in an incredibly annoying voice. No response. SHE takes a breath to sing on.)

Show me your other hand...

(2 holds up her other hand.)

Good, wiggle.

(Wiggles fingers.)

Bend.

(Bends, rather limited, but hard to tell if it's from injury or lack of motivation.)

Uh! Bend again.

(2 bends fingers again, stiff but functional.)

Fair enough.

(2 drops hand.)

1. Now face.

2. No.

1. Come on, campers. Show me face.

2. They didn't go for the face.

1. Then show it to me.

2. Listen. You don't owe me anything.

1. I've got a Tell.

2. I don't care.

1. It's one you never heard before.

2. I don't want to hear it.

1. It's a funny Tell. Funny's best.

2. Then tell it, I don't give a shit.

1. Show me your face first.

2. Go to hell.

1. Show me your face, I'll give you the Tell.

2. Forget it.

1. What's the big secret?

(Pokes **2***'s back with her foot.)*

2. There's no secret, I told you they didn't go for the face! I don't want to talk about it, I don't want to talk to you, it's over, let it go, I'm through. Do me that much.

1. Dream on.

2. Fuck you!

1. In your dreams.

2. You're not doing me any favors!

1. You're so right.

*(***2*** jerks up.)*

2. Look! I don't have to –

(SHE stops, pain lower down.)

1. Okay.

*(***1*** watches her quietly. Gentle now.)*

They went inside, huh? … Breathe.

*(***2*** breathes, a vocal sound escapes.)*

Air.

*(***2*** breathes silently a moment.)*

2. Many.

1. Many?

*(***2*** says nothing.)*

Two?

*(***2*** says nothing.)*

Three?

(Nothing.)

Okay. Straighten your legs.

(*2 obeys.*)

Better?

(*1 allows her a moment.*)

One woman I knew counted up to 25.

2. 25?

1. Yep.

2. Hm-mm.

1. Yeah.

2. Can't be done. After 4 or 5… you lose count.

1. Well maybe she was just weird.

2. She was.

1. You can't remember beyond 4 or 5 and she can recall up to 25.

(*2 settles back, weak, but relaxing.*)

2. She's a better man than I.

1. You're still alive.

2. *(Pleased)* Fuck you.

1. Call 'em as I see 'em.

2. There's a will, there's a way.

1. Over hill and under dale.

2. Rolling stone gathers no moss.

1. A stitch in time.

2. Yeah?

1. What?

2. Finish it.

1. I did.

2. Fuck you, you lose, you don't remember the whole thing.

1. A stitch in time.

2. No. Not the whole thing.

1. That's all there is to it, a stitch in time!

2. Meaning?

1. Meaning… a stitch in time… is a good thing! …

(2 stifles a laugh.)

1. Try to repair the rips early, don't leave the damage, be- cause if you wait 'til later it'll be much worse. A stitch in time.

2. Saves…

1. Trouble. It saves you from later. Unless something worse happens later.

2. You don't have it all, you lose.

1. *(Becoming serious)* There isn't any more, and it's not a contest.

2. You lose.

1. I wasn't competing.

2. You don't know it.

1. I don't really care.

2. Of course not.

1. It's not funny.

2. Okay.

1. You're being mean.

2. 'A stitch in time.'

1. You're very ungracious.

2. Uh-huh.

1. If you have the advantage you can afford to show some grace.

(2 starts working her way toward standing.)

2. Then grace doesn't mean shit. Grace when you can afford it is like water from a tap. Easy. Grace… under pressure… means something.

1. Well you don't have it! …

(1 pushes 2 over with a sudden impetuous foot.

2 lies stunned. Then slowly sits up, her back to 1. A silence.)

What's the rest of it?

(Silence.)

Don't sulk.

(Silence.)

I'm not going to apologize, you were a brat, you deserved it.

(Silence.)

Please tell me. I admit, I don't know 'A stitch in time'... what?

(Silence.)

Please. I'm really sorry. I mean it. Please tell me.

*(**2**'s shoulders start to shake.)*

Please.

*(**2** is laughing.)*

I'll kick you again. I mean it, I don't care. I'll make it number six today!

*(**2** laughs outright.)*

Dammit! ...

(SHE hits the wall.)

Dammit! TELL ME!

(Strikes the wall again, near tears.)

GODAMMIT! I don't hold anything back from you, I'm there when you need me, I'm a person, I deserve the truth!

(Yanking her own chain furiously.)

You bitch! You Goddamn bitch! God, I hate you! I really –

(Suddenly grabs her head.)

Oh...

2. What?

1. Just... faint...

2. Bend.

1. Huh?

(2 turns to look.)

2. Bend. Put your head down.

(1 points.)

1. Hah, got your face.

(2 looks disgusted.)

Open.

(2 acquiesces, opens mouth, showing teeth & jaw.)

Eyes.

(Moves eyes about, showing no damage.)

Neck.

2. Don't push it.

1. Neck.

(2 bends head left, right. 1 is satisfied, and triumphant.)

Hah.

(BOTH sit. The silence grows heavy.)

So. No face today. That's alright.

2. Told you.

1. They worked inside.

2. What's your Tell?

1. Huh-uh.

2. Don't hold out.

1. What's 'A stitch in time'?

2. No way.

1. Okay.

(1 moves away. 2 follows.)

2. It's no trade.

1. Fine.

2. Your Tell is just something I don't know, I never happened to hear your story. But 'A stitch in time' is common knowledge, everybody should know it, but you can't remember, you've lost ground.

1. Go to hell.

2. No, it's not equal, that's all I'm saying. It's not a trade. One is factual information, which you need. The other is just… experiential.

1. My Tell is new information.

2. It's personal.

1. Right, and it's mine! Without me, you'll never have it. I'm the only source.

2. It's just experience, subjective.

1. An old saying can be found in any old book.

2. Huh, oh what a relief.

1. It's a platitude, anybody can get it. Mine's rare. This is the source, baby, come to mama. This is the only place you can get it. Can't get rarer than that….

(*2 wobbles.*)

1. Hang on to something, you're gonna fall over.

2. (*Feigning weakness*) Okay, you win, what is it?

1. Huh, no way.

2. Yeah.

1. You first.

2. (*Giving it up*) No chance! I'll never tell, you can torture my fuckin' brains out!

1. Oh, goody!

(*They laugh. 2 doubles over in pain.*)

2. Oh God!

(*1 watches, pulling remote.*)

1. (*Coolly*) Don't stand up.

(*2 has to bend.*)

2. Something's wrong.

1. Yeah.

2. I mean it, something's hurt.

1. Don't stand up.

2. Fuck you! Don't tell me not to stand up!

1. You do what you want.

2. I don't have room for you.

> (1 *simply turns her back.*)

> You hear me? You hear me, if I go down I –

> (2 *is overcome, has to sink down.*)

1. Moonlight.

2. If I die here –

1. That's the Tell.

2. Moonlight?

1. Listen, don't tell this. When there's a moon, and it's good weather out, I get a shaft of moonlight.

2. You do not.

1. I do, I get a shaft from the moon. A tiny, tiny, weak little beam of moon. But I get it, there's a crack, and I see it.

2. I've never seen it.

1. I've never shown it to you. I've never showed it to anyone.

2. No one before me?

1. I am the only person who's seen it. Unless the person before me.

2. I'm serious, are you telling the truth?

1. *(Genuine)* This is a Tell.

2. How big?

1. Abooout, this big

> *(Holds up fingers.)*

> But it's moonlight. It's a moonbeam.

> (2 *has a pain again.* 1 *moves closer.*)

I fell in a pond once, at night, when I was really little, and it was so incredibly dark it was just black, and completely cold, and without breath and I was, really I was drowning, because I could swim a little but in the dark of this tomb you don't know which way is up. You just feel the water moving around you and you could be going down but you don't know. Because you don't know where the surface is. You know? It was bad.

(2 has stopped shifting around, listening.)

And I was just frozen there, with no air and no hope and no idea which way was up. And then you know what happened?

2. What?

1. This silver sliver nicked my eye and it made me turn my head, this little blinding flash, and I looked and it was a moonbeam shining down through to me. Up through the water I saw the light spreading out and shimmering above me on the surface and I, I, I don't know how, I fought toward it, and I struggled up, and went up, and with my last breath of life I came up into the night air.

(2 has forgotten her pain.)

2. Wow.

1. Isn't that something? I was saved by a moonbeam. I – I was saved. I was saved. By a moonbeam.

2. Is that true?

1. Yes it's true.

2. Romantic.

1. But it happened. And now I have a moonbeam here.

2. Are you gonna swim up to it?

1. Mm-hm. That's how I know I'll be okay.

2. Because you have a moonbeam?

(1 nods.)

I don't have a moonbeam.

(1 gets remote again.)

1. Nothing I can do about that.

2. I wanna be okay.

1. You have to find your own thing.

(2 tries to think of something, looks around, bereft.

THEY are interrupted by a SOUND OFFSTAGE: DIS-TANT, muffled, as behind a door. BOTH come to their feet, staring intently like dogs to a dreaded sound. 1 glances over.)

2. I dunnow.

1. Only one.

2. One comes first sometimes.

(THEY listen. Nothing.)

1. They'll take somebody.

2. Yeah.

1. They took you last.

2. Yeah.

1. They take you twice sometimes.

2. Yeah.

1. Maybe. But probably not.

2. Yeah.

1. Oh God!

(1 retreats, staving off panic.)

2. What color is it?

1. What?

2. The moonbeam.

1. I can't always keep it in my head. When it gets
bad –

2. What color?

1. I try to keep a, keep a really keen picture in my head, of
this little beam, but –

2. What color is the beam?

1. You can, you can, you can keep a picture to a certain
point, but you never know what they're going to do! –

2. Hey.

1. I have to have time in between to get it back! It's not
close enough –

2. I don't care! What color is the moonlight!

1. What?

2. That shines in here.

> *(Another SOUND: STILL FAR. BOTH listen.* **1** *moves to* **2**.*)*

1. Tell me.

2. What?

1. Your Tell.

2. I don't have one.

1. 'A stitch in time.'

2. Oh.

1. Seriously, what's the rest of it?

2. No.

> *(***1** *retreats again.)*

1. Oh God!

2. If it's you, then I'll tell.

1. You will?

2. Just before they take you.

1. Why can't you tell me now?

2. You have a clue.

1. When?

2. Earlier.

1. I don't remember!

2. No, just think.

1. It's too long!

2. Just –

1. Sh!

> *(THEY listen. Nothing.)*

> It's too long, give me the clue again. A stitch in time
> ... *what?*

2. Saves.

1. What?

2. Saves...

1. *What?*

2. A stitch in time saves…

1. …Trouble!

2. That's the clue.

>   *(SOUND: FOOTSTEPS APPROACHING.)*

1. They're here! Tell me now.

2. What color is your moonbeam?

>   *(1's gaze is frozen on the door.)*

>   White or yellow?… White or yellow?

1. Uh…

2. White or yellow!

1. White, it's white. It's yellow!

2. If it's –

>   *(SOUND: FOOTSTEPS JUST OUTSIDE.)*

1. A stitch in time…

2. Not yet.

>   *(SOUND: KEYS RATTLING.)*

1. Tell me.

2. Any minute.

1. Tell me.

2. Just hold on.

>   *(SOUND: KEYS IN DOOR.)*

1. Tell me! Tell me! Tell me!

2. Not 'til you come back.

>   *(1 is stunned. SHE twists it into a spiteful determination.)*

1. Goddamn you!

2. That's right.

>   *(THEY stare at each other, steely, as…*

>   *DOOR IS UNLOCKED.*

>   *BLACKOUT. A BRIEF PAUSE. MUSIC OR PERCUSSION IN THE DARKNESS.)*

PART II

LIGHTS UP:

(2 is sitting still, watching 1.

1 lies crumpled on the floor, her back to 2, severely beaten. [This effect should be communicated through the actor, without the use of special make-up.])

2. Have a nice time did we?

1. ...Uh?

2. Welcome back.

(1 mutters something indecipherable.)

What?

1. Sa'moon?

2. I don't understand you.

(Tries feebly to be clearer.)

1. Th're's a moon?

2. The moon isn't out yet.

1. Can't swim...

2. No swimming. Just lie there.

1. S'save?

2. Your mind is wandering.

1. Wha's save?

2. Bring your mind back.

1. 'Ell me.

2. What?

1. Stitch.

2. Oh man. Can you sit up?

1. Wha's save?

2. Are you hurt?

1. Stitch.

2. Show me your hands.

1. Tell me.

2. Do this first. Show me your hands.

(1 slides out a damaged hand.)

Okay, wiggle.

(Tries to comply.)

Not bad. Bend.

(Same, not good.)

Okay, very good.

1. Nuh.

2. Yes it is, if I say it is.

1. S'bad.

2. I'm the one who can see. And I'm saying, no problem. Don't sweat it.

1. Got kicked.

2. Show me face.

1. Kicked.

2. It hurts worse than it is, just show it to me.

(1 shows her battered head.

2 conceals her reaction.)

Alright, not bad. Not bad at all. Mouth.

(1 lays her head down.)

1. Tell me.

2. You didn't do mouth.

1. I need to know.

2. I need to see.

1. Then you tell.

2. Okay.

(Nothing. 1 still doesn't move.)

Maybe.

1. *Maybe!*

(This fires 1 into rolling over.)

2. In a little while.

(1 begins the arduous task of sitting up.)

1. *Maybe* you lie.

2. I told you I'd tell.

1. Said that before.

2. Let's see the neck.

1. Maybe you held out.

2. So you'd come back.

1. Maybe they kick me.

2. You came back.

1. Maybe they wanted to kill me.

2. You're back.

1. Maybe I told.

2. Told?

1. Yeah.

2. Told what?

1. They ask questions.

2. I know, but we never have any answers.

1. Maybe they got a gun.

2. Maybe they did, it doesn't make us know anything. Maybe they'll shoot you, what're you gonna do?

1. Tell.

2. You don't know anything! If you did you'd've told 'em before all this fucking shit happened. What'd you do, make something up?

1. No.

2. Then what can you tell them?

1. That you do.

2. What?

1. Maybe I told them you knew something.

2. I don't think so.

1. Maybe.

2. You didn't say that.

(1 *feels her head gingerly.*)

1. I got a headache.

2. I don't believe you.

1. I do, I have a headache.

2. Fuck you, you didn't tell them that.

1. My lips hurt too.

2. Why would you tell them I know something?

1. You do.

2. I do not!

1. I asked, but you wouldn't tell.

(2 's turn to be stunned.)

2. What?

1. You held out.

2. Jesus Christ, it's just a fucking Tell!

1. I feel bad, do I look as bad as I feel?

2. Oh my God!

1. You tell me the truth.

2. I'm serious, this isn't a joke, you can't tell them something like that!

1. How do I look?

(2 looks at door, beginning to panic.)

2. If they think I know something... I don't know what they're gonna do... !

1. Tell me.

(2 is overtaken, tries hysterically to get loose.)

2. I don't deserve to die here!

(1 just watches.)

Please!

1. You tell me what I look like.

(2's panic dies to a slow burn.)

2. Oh man, you deserve what you got.

1. So will you.

(THEY stare at each other.)

2. You look completely fucked up.

1. Yeah?

2. Yeah.

1. Not what you said.

2. I lied.

1. Liar.

2. S'cuse me for trying to cut you a break!

1. You lie.

2. So do you! At least you better be.

1. Go on. Go on!

2. Your nose looks broken.

1. Bad?

2. Not if you're a cauliflower fan.

1. Go on.

2. Your head's busted and your eyes are fucked up, the right one.

1. Swollen or cut?

2. More like pulp.

1. Skip the commentary.

2. Your lips are bad. There's some blood around your ear, and there's a lot of blood coming from your mouth.

1. From the lips?

2. No, from inside. I'd say you broke some teeth.

1. Broke…

2. Teeth, that's what I said, broken teeth.

1. How many?

2. You want me to count?

1. Fuck you.

2. Your hands are a mess.

1. I can see my hands. What's the lips?

2. Nothing stitches and surgery won't fix.

1. Uh.

2. You know what they say. 'A stitch in time…'

1. Say the rest of it!

2. I wouldn't tell you now if my life depended on it!

1. Maybe it does.
2. Maybe it doesn't.
1. Maybe it does. Go on.
2. That's head and hands, I don't know about the rest. I don't know if they worked insi –
1. No.
2. No?
1. They didn't.
2. Lucky dog.
1. Lucky me.
2. Lucky charm.
1. Lucky… rabbit's foot.
2. Lucky four leaf clover.

   (1 *tries to shift, flinches.*)

1. Rib…
2. Lucky rib?
1. Think I broke it…
2. Not so lucky.
1. Go on.
2. Fuck you.
1. Fuck you.
2. No, fuck you, fuckin' bitch.
1. Bite me.
2. Go to hell.
1. Kiss my ass.
2. Suck my dick, asswipe fucking bitch asshole!
1. Cunt.
2. Cocksucking whore.
1. Motherfucker.
2. Fuckwad!
1. Prick!
2. Eat my shit!
1. Fuck yourself!

2. Shitlicker!

1. Fart-fucker!

2. Dickhead!

1. Douchebag!

2. Needle-dick!

1. F – Sh – Cocksucker!

2. I said that!

1. I said it, bitch!

2. I said that too!

1. Say this!

> (1 *tries to flip her the finger, has to switch hands.* 2 *laughs.*)

2. Well well, one finger still works.

> (*BOTH laugh.*)

1. Tit-head.

2. Tit-head? That's deep. That and "fart-fucker," I like those two.

1. You are those two.

> (2 *suffers a pain. As SHE turns,* 1 *sees the back of her pants.*)

> Hey, you're bleeding.

2. Fuck you, slut.

1. Whore.

2. Hooker.

1. Tramp.

2. Cunt-on-the-punt.

> (*SHE tries to retreat victorious, but the pain worsens.*)

1. How long have you been bleeding?

2. Stalling won't help. Cheater.

1. Liar.

2. Murderer.

1. Right.

2. If you told them… what you said…

1. How long have you been bleeding?

2. *You're* bleeding.

1. I'm supposed to be bleeding.

2. What, you cornered the market?

1. Right, it's my turn to lose blood.

> (**2** *sinks down.*)

2. I'd feel a whole lot better if you just tell me what you said to them.

1. So would I. Why don't we just tell each other?

2. I'll tell you if you tell me.

1. I'll tell you if you stop bleeding.

2. Please *don't*, I don't want to play anymore! It's not a game, I don't want to die here!

1. Okay. Look, you tell me your Tell and I'll tell you my Tell.

2. Yours is not a Tell, it's just the truth! All I'm asking for is the truth!

> (*The pain worsens.*)

Oh! Oh, make it stop!

1. Okay –

> (**1** *tries to get to her but isn't able.*)

2. It's really bad!

1. Here, give me your hand.

2. Oh God, make it stop!

1. Reach out your hand to me!

2. Please do something!

> (*Lacking anything else,* **1** *leans in and uses dead earnest.*)

1. Okay. Listen. You want the truth? Here it is.

2. Oh...

1. The truth is, I'm played out and you're probably hemorrhaging.

2. What... ?

1. We're not gonna get saved.

2. No, don't –

1. Whether we die in their hands or in this room is just a detail.

2. We… have…

1. The truth is, we're all we have, and we don't even know each other's names.

2. Moonbeam… !

1. I made it up.

2. Tell me the moonbeam!

1. I lied.

2. Please!

1. You want the truth, tell me your name.

2. No!

1. Why not?

2. Forget it.

1. Someone should know it.

2. Not that!

1. Tell me a Tell!

2. Fuck off!

1. Give me a Tell before you die.

2. Not telling!

1. Why not?

2. I don't want it!

1. Why not!

2. I don't want it!

> *(Pulling herself off the floor.)*

> You can't have it! You can shoot me or cut me or fuck me to death or whatever it is they'll do, I don't give a shit, that'll be the end of this shell and thank God for worms and maggots! But nobody will have killed me. Because *I* was never here. This room never heard my name. The first time they did those things to me, it wasn't me anymore. I am not the kind of person this happens to. And what you see here, isn't me.

(SHE looks off.)

It… it ripped out of my body and flew away, *shuuu*! Far away! She's gone. She's got the name. And they've got nothing.

*(**2** comes back to herself slowly.*

1 *coughs and winces. SHE is lying on the floor, spent.)*

You look…

1. What?

2. A little peakéd.

1. I'm very thirsty.

2. I don't have anything.

1. I know.

2. If I did I would give it to you.

1. If you did… I would kiss you.

2. I would let you.

*(**2** rests weakly against wall. **1** doesn't move.)*

1. I'm glad.

2. Hm?

1. That she got free.

2. She got lost.

1. You might find her again.

2. You shouldn't've given up your moonbeam.

1. You wanted the truth.

2. I needed the moonbeam.

1. You are a fool.

2. Why?

*(**1** is lying still.)*

I'm not a fool for loving your beautiful moonbeam.

1. You never needed it. Dork.

2. It was what we had.

1. I still have my name.

2. And what do I have?

(*1 Doesn't answer.*)

What do I have?

(*1's eyes are closed.*)

Hey! Fuck you, don't doze off on me. Tit-head!

1. Mm…

2. C'mere. …

(*2 crawls to the end of her chain and extends a leg.*)

2. … Not gonna have you spacing. Come lie on my leg.
C'mon.

1. Too far.

2. Don't make me sing.

(*2 SINGS in annoying voice, copying 1's song from earlier. Nothing.*)

Come on. Lie on me, my leg is out. 'No time like the
present!'

(*1 struggles to respond.*)

1. Never put off to tomorrow…

2. What you can do today. Good. A penny saved…

1. Penny earned.

2. Okay, but you should come over here.

(*1 doesn't answer.*)

Okay, that's alright, your turn. No stalling. Stalling for
time is cheating.

(*1 makes a soft sound.*)

Uh uh, A man may work from sun to sun…

1. (*Mumbling*) Woman's work, never done.

2. Yes, okay. My go. All's fair…

(*No reply.*)

C'mon. All's fair in love…

(*Kicks 1's arm.*)

Hey! I'm not gonna let you lose, now come on!

(1 opens her eyes.)

I'm not gonna let you. …

(1 ever-so-slowly begins to move.)

That's right.

(1 rolls onto her stomach.)

Good. Come on.

(1 places her forearms on the floor, and pulls herself toward 2's leg, using the words.)

1. A stitch…

(Another pull.)

In time…

(One more.)

Saves…

(2 scoots down to meet her, 1 rolls over onto her leg.)

2. You made it.

1. Mm.

2. Better?

1. I think you better tell me.

(2 studies her, tries to judge it.)

2. Why am I a fool for loving your beautiful moonbeam?

1. Not gonna tell me, are you?

2. The moonlight was real. It was your thing.

1. No.

(Familiar SOUND OUTSIDE: DISTANT. 2 looks up, terrified.)

2. They're coming!

1. Hey. Don't worry.

2. You never told them I knew anything.

1. But I told *you.*

2. *(Tenderly)* You're such a liar.

1. It was just words. But you bought it.

2. Cheaters never prosper.

    (ANOTHER SOUND.)

1. No, listen. That's your thing. Words. The moonbeam was just a story. You're such a sucker for a Tell. The moonlight is in your mind.

    (SOUND: CLOSER.)

2. Listen. I have a Tell for you.

1. Mm.

2. You'll like this, it's a word. Are you ready?

1. What?…

2. A stitch in time sav –

1. No.

2. But –

1. No!

    (SOUND: FOOTSTEPS APPROACHING.)

2. If they take me I –

1. Save it.

2. Just let me –

1. Save it.

2. Please!

1. *(Faint) S*ave it, save it… save it….

2. Alright. For you. I'm saving it.

    *(***1*** dies.*

    SOUND: JUST OUTSIDE.)

    I'm saving it…

    (SOUND: KEYS JANGLING.

    2 *gently lays* **1** *down, and gets to her knees.)*

    I'm saving it.

    (SHE stands. Faces door, as it is heard UNLOCKING.)

    I'm saving it.

    (BLACKOUT.)

COMMENCING

Kate Bennis and Colleen Davenport

SETTING

A modest apartment in the city.

TIME

50 minutes.

ROLES

KELLI – Smart, witty, straight. Prone to rants.
ARLIN – Smart, witty, gay. Fond of diatribes.

(MUSIC: A great song! It morphs from the opening music to the stereo in **KELLI**'s apartment, a nice place, but not expensive.*

***AT RISE:** A KNOCK on the door.* **KELLI** hurries out, looking smashing, putting on earrings. Turns OFF MUSIC, checks her watch, her look, grabs jacket, answers door. SHE stops.*

A WOMAN in a parka stands holding an elaborate bouquet.)

KELLI. Oh…

ARLIN. Hi.

KELLI. I was expecting someone else.

ARLIN. If I had a nickel.

KELLI. Sorry?

ARLIN. Kelli Sloan?

KELLI. Oh, flowers! Those are beautiful! – Oh God, I'm such a gleeb, come on in! I bet I know who those are from!

ARLIN. Well –

KELLI. Arlin, right?

ARLIN. You got it.

KELLI. Wow! Let me get my wallet.

ARLIN. Sure.

*(**KELLI** returns with her purse.)*

KELLI. Those are just magnificent!

ARLIN. Hothouse Lilies.

KELLI. Wow, expensive!

(Taking flowers.)

This is a *very good* start! This is *very* promising!

ARLIN. Really?

KELLI. I have a hot date tonight and this is really classy!

(*Hands her bills.*)

I don't know what you get, is five okay?

ARLIN. Uh –

KELLI. Oh, take a ten! I have a very good feeling about tonight and you've been my lucky charm.

ARLIN. I don't think so.

KELLI. No, go ahead!

ARLIN. I'm definitely not lucky.

KELLI. Well, take it anyway, maybe your luck will change, mine did.

ARLIN. Well if –

KELLI. No, really! I haven't had a date in six months, I haven't slept with a man in nine, and tonight, not only have I lost ten pounds and fit this dress again but, because of a friend at the office, I have a blind date with a guy who sends me very expensive hothouse flowers! So, I am feeling the tides turning and so must you! Take the ten *and* this twenty, and when you get off work take somebody out and buy them some really expensive flowers! Okay?

(**KELLI** *sees* **ARLIN** *to the door.*)

ARLIN. I already did.

KELLI. Okay then! Good luck!

ARLIN. I bought those flowers.

KELLI. Well, good choice, worked for me! And thanks again.

ARLIN. Um…Your date…

KELLI. Wait a minute! Don't say anything else! He's not coming, is he?

ARLIN. It's, it –

KELLI. So these are because –

(*Grabs bouquet, heading for trash can.*)

Oh no, no no no! If this guy is too chickenshit to

even –

(Can't trash 'em, veers off.)

Ya know what? I am *so* gonna kill Maria tomorrow! I *told* her I wasn't – Oo, I am gonna kill her and hang her fucking head out the office window for the crows to come and peck out her eyeballs, and she and her friends, who had this guy who was so nice, that would be so 'perfect' for me, they can just stick it in their ears and pull their brains out the other side, because I'm sorry, I can just live without this!

*(Pushes flowers at **ARLIN**.)*

Would you, I'm sorry, could you just please just take these back to their point of origin and, give them to somebody, an orphanage or something, because I don't want them, I'm sorry, thank you, I just don't need this, I don't need them, I don't need shithead blind dates, and I don't need sex! I'll become a nun, or move to fucking Alaska where it's legal to have sex with dogs!

(Tries to pull up pantyhose, ends up tearing them.)

God, I give up, I dunnow why I try! I hate panty hose anyway. Really, I give up!

*(Flops down on the couch. **ARLIN** is still standing there.)*

Show's over, you can go now.

ARLIN. A lot of this is because I have a hard time speaking up.

KELLI. What?

ARLIN. I gave you the wrong impression.

KELLI. Don't tell me he *is* coming, I already screwed up my pantyhose. What, he's coming late?

ARLIN. No. Worse than that.

KELLI. What?

*(THEY stare at each other. **KELLI** finally gets it.)*

No.

ARLIN. Apparently.

KELLI. You?

(**ARLIN** *nods.*)

You're Arlin? The *date* Arlin? My blind date that Maria sent, for me, that everybody thought would be such a good match? Oh, this is a *good* day. This is really nice. So now no guy is showing up, and at least one person in the office thinks I'm a lesbian!

ARLIN. Oh, how horrible.

KELLI. No offense, but I'm not a lesbian.

ARLIN. No offense, but I am.

KELLI. Did Maria tell you that? Where did she get that? I don't act like that! Did she tell your friends I was gay? Because I'm not! – I mean we joke around, but – What did they tell you about me, I mean precisely?

ARLIN. Well, goodbye.

KELLI. Wait. Wait a minute, I'm sorry. I just need to ask. Did you think I was a lesbian?

ARLIN. Well, I'd love to stay and prolong this, but I think it would be more fun to go on home & shoot off four or five toes.

KELLI. I'm sorry. Um, look, obviously this is very awkward for us both. You should, you should, you should at least take these flowers with you.

ARLIN. That's okay –

KELLI. No really, they're really expensive looking, you should –

(*Pushes flowers into her hands,* **ARLIN** *out door.*)

ARLIN. You –

KELLI. Really, it would be best, thank you.

ARLIN. Look, I just –

KELLI. Thanks. Sorry, I just –

ARLIN. I don't have anyone I –

KELLI. I'm just really sorry this happened, another time maybe – I mean no, um, bye!

(**KELLI** *closes door on* **ARLIN** *and cringes.*)

Oooh my Goood! I want to die! That was so excruciat-ing! Oh my God!

(*Picks up phone & dials.*)

Oh, man! What *was* that!

(*Into phone*)

Lees, hi it's me, *worst* date night of all time! Blind date, from the office, comes to the door, it's a *woman*!! Somebody set me up with a *woman*, can you believe it! (*Screams*) AAAAA! Could you die?! Call me!

(*Dialing again.*)

Oh my God, I just need to smell some male pheromones or –

(*Into phone*)

Chaz, Kelli, hi, could you die? Maria Fuentes set me up with a blind date tonight, and it was a LESBIAN! AAAGH! Oh, ick, the apartment is just full of icky sex vibes! …

(*A KNOCK on the door, SHE freezes. Whispering…*)

Someone at the door. Could be the lesbian, gotta go, call me!

(*Hangs up, stands frozen. Another KNOCK, LOUDER.* **KELLI** *answers it.*)

Hi –

(**ARLIN** *bursts in, throwing flowers at* **KELLI**.)

ARLIN. Here! Those are yours! I bought them for you, and even if you don't want them you can at least have the good grace to pretend until I'm out of sight, they were a gift, and whether or not you want or like a gift, everyone has the right to have something graciously received, even if it's only for show and you throw them out later! It's a courtesy!

(**ARLIN** *stomps OUT. SHE stomps back IN. Throws*

money.)

And here! This is your twenty and your ten! The most *not-worth-it* tip I ever got in my life!

(SHE stomps OUT. Stomps back IN.)

And I don't know who you are that you should be so narrow minded about *who* your date turns out to be! What if I'd been a handsome guy who just wasn't that bright, or a really handsome guy who showed up in a wheelchair – or what if I'd been an ugly guy, but with a genuinely handsome '65 Mustang convertible? And as it turned out I wasn't a guy at all – though I am relatively handsome, not that you'd notice, prancing around ripping your panty hose – but it's just a shame is all, because we could have laughed about this and gone to dinner anyway – you do go to dinner with friends don't you? – and had a pretty decent time of it and maybe even salvaged this evening. But no –

KELLI. Look –

ARLIN. – if you weren't *so* overcome with who does & does not have icky sex vibes – !

KELLI. Oh, God.

ARLIN. – which, by the way, is not *me*, babe, I'll clue ya, 'cause I haven't had sex in even longer than *you*! Although I will say, in my own defense, if & when I do ever have sex again, it will not be icky, which is more than I can say for you, judging by the way you treat people!

*(**ARLIN** turns and EXITS.)*

KELLI. Hey!

(Shouting down hall.)

Hey, Godammit!

ARLIN. What!

KELLI. I'm not taking the shit for this!

*(**ARLIN** stomps back IN.)*

I'm not the bad guy here! Why didn't you just say

something!

ARLIN. I was trying!

KELLI. Well, you didn't have to stand there! You could've stopped me!

ARLIN. I'm not the verbal police! And you have eyes!

KELLI. You're a woman, in a big parka, which of those is supposed to tell me you're my date?

ARLIN. This is my coat, what do you wear? I suppose you have some incredibly cute little "date coat."

KELLI. Don't make fun of me! Yes, I dress for occasions.

ARLIN. So did I, it's under my coat! And *I* blew 30 bucks on flowers.

KELLI. Yea, well, the flowers were nice...Why didn't you just say you were the date?

ARLIN. I was a little taken aback, okay? I'm not accustomed to being handed a tip in the first ten seconds that I meet someone.

KELLI. Oh.

ARLIN. The following morning maybe. A little something for exceptional service.

(Pause.)

That's a joke.

KELLI. I know.

ARLIN. Fine.

(Awkward pause.)

KELLI. I do have a date coat.

(Holds up little jacket.)

It's not real warm. I'm always cold on dates. But then later you tell him – your date I mean –

ARLIN. Yes I know.

KELLI. You tell the guy you're chilly, and then they put their coat around you, and that can lead to some very cozy moments.

ARLIN. Right.

KELLI. You ever done that?

ARLIN. Which? Put my coat around a woman, or been the chilly one?

KELLI. The chilly one.

ARLIN. I think one of the most asinine things you can do is go out, ostensibly to have fun, and purposely wear something that makes you uncomfortable.

KELLI. Oh.

ARLIN. Not so much you personally, but straight women in general – especially femmy straight women, or femmy gay women, well, guys do it too – even a dyke'll do it once in a while if they're really smitten bad – but really, the worst is straight women: you wear those little tight clothes & those little tight hose, & the little pointy shoes & the teeny little butt & tiny little waist, and pretty soon you're just so teeny-tiny we could put you on a little shelf & look at you through an itty bitty microscope! I mean, if you're gonna go out & hang loose & live large, how can you do that when you're trying to be such a teeny-weeny little pin-size person?

(Pause. **KELLI** *looks at her.)*

KELLI. It wouldn't hurt you to get a coat.

ARLIN. Okay, that's fair. But if I can just say this, it wouldn't hurt you to get a decent pair of shoes with some support.

KELLI. I hate, hate flats!

ARLIN. I'm not talking about doinky orthopedic clodhoppers, just don't teeter around in those little pin-pricks.

KELLI. I love to teeter.

ARLIN. Foreshortens your calf muscles.

KELLI. Men love it when you teeter.

ARLIN. Oh, they sure do. It's just so sexy when a woman is struggling at all times just to keep her balance in this world. Oh, that is so sexy.

KELLI. Uh-huh.

ARLIN. 'Maybe she'll fall over & I can help her up. Gee, I can only hope.'

KELLI. You like that, do you?

ARLIN. Me? I like to help people up if they're down, yes. Do I like people to feign weakness to make me feel strong? No, I don't. Do I like women to look great, yes. Do I want them to wear tight little clothes so I can ogle them? N – well –

KELLI. Ah-hah!

ARLIN. Only if they're comfortable! And not cold! I don't need some woman shrink-wrapping herself. But, y'know, if she wants to wear something pleasantly form fitting, that, that could be a good thing.

KELLI. What about this, is this 'teeny tiny tight' or could it be a good thing?

ARLIN. Um…

(**KELLI** *shows it off, not entirely unsexily.*)

KELLI. Tragically tight? Am I compromised?

ARLIN. What?

KELLI. I dunnow, is my freedom compromised by this mini?

ARLIN. It's, um, pretty small.

KELLI. So you don't like it?

ARLIN. Uh…

KELLI. Or, you don't approve?

ARLIN. I – what do you want me to say here!

KELLI. If you were a man you wouldn't want to take me out?

ARLIN. I'm a woman and I wanted to take you out!

KELLI. So you get the point!

ARLIN. What point are we proving?! That you look sexy? That you have a beautiful body? Nobody ever argued, point made, alright?

KELLI. Well, that wasn't exactly the point.

ARLIN. What was the point?

KELLI. Aren't you hot in that parka?

ARLIN. Was the point to see if I find you sexy?

KELLI. The point, I dunnow – God, men are a lot less draining to talk to, all you have to do is listen! I don't even know what the hell the subject was – The point was, you were ragging on women for wearing tight clothes & I was just saying there's a good reason to wear them, point made, dig a hole, bury it, goodbye!

ARLIN. Why do straight women like to do that?

KELLI. Oh, what?

ARLIN. Come on to lesbians.

KELLI. Oh, right!

ARLIN. You don't want to sleep with us, but there's a little part of you that just can't resist trying to see if we find you attractive. Just to see.

KELLI. That is outrageous! And why are *you* allowed to make these generalizations, I'd like to know! How come if *I* say, "You lesbians love coming on to straight women," it sounds like a horrible ignorant stereotype! But if *you* say, "Straight women love coming on to gays," it comes off like some hip, witty little insight! Why are you allowed to get away with that?

ARLIN. Gee I dunnow, maybe it's compensation for those last couple centuries, where you had a tendency to beat, burn and kill us!

KELLI. You must be a really fun date.

ARLIN. That's all the Salem witches were you know, lesbians and herbal healers.

KELLI. What?

ARLIN. Yeah. And it hasn't been that long since it was still legally a mental illness. And they could do anything, have you committed, perform lobotomies, sterilize you, whatever! Ancient history, right? Except right now in Connecticut there's a case pending of a woman trying to regain custody of her son, which she lost simply for being a lesbian!

KELLI. Uh-huh.

ARLIN. Oh, you think you're so safe 'cause you're straight! Well under the Nazis in Germany, a woman had to bear children to even be considered a citizen!

KELLI. What?

ARLIN. No baby, no citizenship! And just bear in mind, here in the real modern world, the Constitution of our country doesn't officially include you or me! Only all *men* are created equal –

KELLI. S'cuse me...

ARLIN. – Second class citizen? No! Just because women are still paid less for the same work, we would only be protected if we had an Equal Rights Amendment, which we don't! You know what we have to protect us? Men!

KELLI. S'cuse me!

ARLIN. – The same ones who're hoping you'll fall over so they can help you up!

KELLI. S'cuse me, s'cuse me!

ARLIN. Sorry!

KELLI. Man, that is a diatribe! Earth to person, lighten up! Take a pill or something. And you better either leave or take off that parka 'cause you're so red you look like you're gonna explode. You want some water or something?

(**ARLIN** *nods yes.* **KELLI** *gets it.*)

Look, I am not that much of a feminist or political or anything, okay? And I'll be really frank with you, there is something seriously unattractive about a woman going off like that, okay? It's like, please don't foist your issues on me, alright, frankly? There's a lot wrong with the world but I'm not gonna carry it all on my shoulders, I have my hands full just trying to get through the fray, one day at a time, one issue at a time, one crisis at a time! – Really, you should take that thing off. – I never seem to have the nerve to say to people, when they do this to me, please, I don't want to know about your beliefs! I'm not gonna fight against the war, and free the rebels, or preserve the, I dunnow, children-building-pandas-school-yard-bunnies, or save the entire planet, sorry! I already have my hands full just trying to have a life & a job & few friends, and make enough money, and maybe even, God forbid, one day have a man in my life again, and in my bed, please God, amen!

(Pause.)

ARLIN. You said yourself you hated panty hose.

KELLI. What? Que, como, quando?

ARLIN. When you were having a tizzy about your date not showing up…

KELLI. I hate the word 'tizzy.'

ARLIN. You said you'd become a nun or move to Alaska where it's legal to have sex with dogs.

KELLI. God, what do you, take notes?

ARLIN. So why do you wear them on dates, to go out and have fun, why would you wear something you don't like?

KELLI. To attract men! So I'll look sexy! Que pasa?!

ARLIN. Why do you have to be uncomfortable to be attractive?

KELLI. That's just the nature of dressing up, okay?

ARLIN. But it's not! I'm dressed up & I'm comfortable!

KELLI. In that parka?!

ARLIN. What you wear is not the point, you'd look sexy in a sweat suit, with mud, and snowshoes.

KELLI. Well, thank you, but what is the point?

ARLIN. I gotta take my coat off.

KELLI. Hello!

(SHE takes it off.)

ARLIN. I'm not gonna stay or anything.

KELLI. Well good, because I don't think we're going to come to a deeper understanding through love and laughter.

ARLIN. Good because I don't wanna understand you.

KELLI. Or you, yeez, that stuff about Nazi women?

(Seeing outfit)

Look at you, you did dress up. Very natty.

*(**ARLIN** looks at her.)*

ARLIN. Is that a joke?

KELLI. No, and it's not a come-on either. It's an observation. I couldn't see your clothes under that parka, now I've seen them and commented. Since you have actually taken the coat off, you might as well actually sit down.

ARLIN. But what?

KELLI. But what what?

ARLIN. I look "very natty." It sounds like a compliment with an implicit 'but.'

KELLI. Look, this is going in one of those directions. Would you like a drink, a real drink, now that you're all re-hydrated?

(Goes to bar area.)

ARLIN. Oh. Uh, yeah. Okay.

KELLI. A drink drink?

ARLIN. A pleasant beverage.

KELLI. That means no alcohol?

ARLIN. Right.

KELLI. Well then I guess we're not going to get drunk and frolic.

(SHE stops.)

Okay, that *was* sort of a flirtatious thing. Weird! Club soda okay?

ARLIN. Thank you.

KELLI. Ice?

ARLIN. Please.

KELLI. You chew it?

ARLIN. Sometimes.

KELLI. Means you're sexually frustrated.

ARLIN. Ding ding, late news flash.

(**KELLI** *brings her drink.*)

KELLI. Man, that was kind of flirty too, wasn't it? Maybe you're right about the sexual come-on thing.

ARLIN. Thanks.

(*SHE drinks. Awkward pause.*)

I should be taking off pretty quick.

KELLI. You have a pressing date, do you?

ARLIN. Right, to chew ice. No, y'know, I should just, get outta here pretty soon.

KELLI. Don't get all shy on me now, dudette, you've thrown stuff at me and had a feminist tizzy in my living room. Don't get all weird now just 'cause you took off your parka.

ARLIN. Doesn't this feel sort of date-like all of a sudden?

KELLI. No, but you can put the coat back on if you need to.

ARLIN. Y'know, those awkward moments at the start of dates.

KELLI. Yeah, especially blind dates. What's your name again? Harley?

ARLIN. Arlin. Why?

KELLI. What is that?

ARLIN. Just a weird name. My mother picked it. So it would be different.

KELLI. It's just funny, because Arlin could be a man or a woman's name, and you're…

ARLIN. A man or a woman?

KELLI. That came out bad, forget I brought it up. I'm gonna have a real drink now, do you mind?

ARLIN. Speaking from my masculine or feminine side?

KELLI. Alright, shuttup, next subject. You don't mind if I drink?

ARLIN. No.

KELLI. Oh good. Because some people, if they're officially "non-drinkers," they can't handle it if you wanna have any fun.

ARLIN. Well I can, so have fun.

KELLI. Are you officially a non-drinker?

ARLIN. Mm-hm.

KELLI. Are you alcoholic?

ARLIN. Yes.

KELLI. Man. I'm sorry, I can't believe I just asked you that. Really, I apologize, I just, for some reason, things come blurting out of my mouth with you that I would never normally say. It's really weird. Anyway, I'm sorry.

(SHE goes back into kitchen.)

So, how did you know you were alcoholic?

ARLIN. I drank too much.

KELLI. Well how much was that?

ARLIN. Every day.

KELLI. Well, lots of people drink everyday.

ARLIN. Lots of people are alcoholics.

KELLI. Did you mess up your life?

ARLIN. Can I have some more club soda?

KELLI. Sure.

ARLIN. Do you have any flavors?

KELLI. Raspberry.

ARLIN. Yeah. Are you afraid you drink too much? Is that why you're asking?

(No answer comes from the kitchen.)

Kelli?

KELLI. *(returning)* Here. Raspberry, lots of ice.

ARLIN. I'll need it.

KELLI. Can I ask you a question?

ARLIN. Yes apparently you can, almost non-stop.

KELLI. I'm sorry, am I being bad?

ARLIN. Well, no, it's...You're very up-front, that kind of honesty is really rare on a first date – Although this is not date.

KELLI. Well, maybe that's why it's easier, because it's not.

ARLIN. Right. Although I wouldn't say there's a complete lack of sexual tension.

KELLI. Huh?

ARLIN. Well, you know, you're an attractive person. For a straight woman.

KELLI. Well, thank you. And I'm sure you're very nice for a lesbian.

(Pause.)

Wow, all of a sudden this does feel like a date.

(Moves)

Can I freshen your soda?

ARLIN. No, it's still flesh – *Fresh!* Wow. Thank you.

KELLI. I'm definitely having a drink. You're sure you don't mind?

ARLIN. Nope. What'cha gonna have?

KELLI. Well, my blind date blew apart and I'm spending the evening with a perfectly nice alcoholic lesbian, I think that rates...Johnnie Walker.

(Silence. SHE looks at ARLIN.)

I meant that jovially.

(ARLIN doesn't reply.)

I'm sorry. I was just being dry. Don't mind what I say....

(ARLIN puts down her drink and gets her parka.)

KELLI. What? Oh come on, don't do that, I didn't mean anything. Don't go away angry – what's your name?

ARLIN. Arlin!

KELLI. Arlin, come on! Things have been blurting out of

my mouth all night, we've been insulting each other for the last half hour. You just said I was attractive "for a straight woman." Don't get pissed off, I don't even know what I said. Really.

(ARLIN goes to door.)

ARLIN. You're an asshole.

KELLI. I am, I'm a real asshole. 'For a straight woman.'

ARLIN. I give up! I don't know what to make of you! One minute you're mincing around flirting, and the next you're insulting me. You want to get rid of me, you want me to stay; you want to know about me, you don't. You're smart and funny and very witty, and then suddenly out comes this ignorant *shit*. I don't know whether I'm coming or going! – Literally!

KELLI. I didn't mean to offend you.

ARLIN. I don't know whether you did or not. I'm not sure you know.

KELLI. Look. The thing is, I just don't know whether you're coming on to me or not. And I just have no idea how to respond, you know, because I don't know what's what.

ARLIN. If I was coming on to you, you would know it! If at any point I thought, "Kelli's the one I want to get in the sack tonight!" I guarantee, you would get the message! I mean, I'm not Casanova, but I would raise a pink flag or something!

KELLI. God, don't be mad. I'm just being honest.

ARLIN. Well trust me, I'm not putting the moves on you!

KELLI. Okay.

ARLIN. I'm not so weak & feeble that I can't even send out a clear sexual signal!

KELLI. Well it's good you're secure.

ARLIN. I have walked into a bar and picked up a woman without ever having to say a word!

KELLI. Really?

ARLIN. There was no confusing my signals anywhere along

the way, okay? I mean, pardon my saying, she had no complaints.

KELLI. Are you serious?

ARLIN. Yes.

KELLI. You took somebody home from a bar without ever having to say anything?

ARLIN. Well, not home, but yeah, hardly a word.

KELLI. And you had this whole affair?

ARLIN. It was short.

KELLI. A short, silent affair.

ARLIN. Shorter.

KELLI. Oh, well, everybody has one night stands.

ARLIN. Shorter, actually.

KELLI. Well how short could it be? You do actually have to find the person & go have sex?

ARLIN. Kinda wish we hadn't gotten into this.

KELLI. Too late.

ARLIN. Well…eventually people needed to get in and…use the facilities.

KELLI. The bathroom?! You had sex in a bar bathroom? I don't even know whether that's cool or kinky or just plain icky! What was it for you?

ARLIN. Um…All three I guess. In that order. First you think it'll be really cool, and then it's pretty kinky, and in the end you realize it was just plain icky.

KELLI. Well was this –

ARLIN. I don't really remember it that well.

KELLI. No?

(**ARLIN** *shakes her head. Holds out her empty glass.*)

ARLIN. Any other flavors?

KELLI. Raspberry or straight – no pun intended.

(*SHE takes glass, goes to refill it.*)

Still, a bathroom in a bar, it just seems like kind of a sexy idea. Raw.

ARLIN. I suppose, as an idea, it is.

KELLI. Yeah?

ARLIN. The reality is that you both stink like cigarettes & booze, and don't know what the other person likes, and you're trying to stand up, and breathing in the smell of urine & farts & those cheap air fresheners, and neither of you wants to get on the germy floor or get your clothes wet. And you do something totally personal with an absolute stranger, and when you're done, you haven't become more intimate with her, you're just, more of a stranger to yourself.

KELLI. Wow.

(KELLI is standing there with the full glass. ARLIN reaches for it.)

ARLIN. Thank you.

KELLI. Sure.

(SHE goes to get herself another drink..)

ARLIN. Drinking really adds to that feeling.

KELLI. What feeling?

ARLIN. Of being a stranger to yourself. Feeling like an alien in the world. That you're marooned on a planet where the gravity doesn't fit you.

(Takes KELLI's drink, looks at it.)

Where everybody else seems nicely grounded, and you try to fit, but you're always either lumbering around, pulled down by everything around you, or else you're hovering just above, too light weight to even register. Trying to make conversation while you're in imminent danger of drifting away. At the first careless remark you'll get blown off into space, to float alone forever. And sometimes you almost wish it would go ahead and happen, so you could at least have the quiet of floating in the dark.

(KELLI takes her drink back.)

KELLI. Well Jesus Christ, if that's how drinking makes you feel why on earth would you ever want to do it?

ARLIN. Because, at the time it feels like the only thing helping you to stand the gravity.

KELLI. Well, it just gives me a nice little glow.

ARLIN. And the main thing is, the one thing you know for sure, is that the drinking is *not* the problem.

KELLI. I'm not an alcoholic, Arlin.

ARLIN. Okay. I was just saying.

KELLI. It's not a problem for me, okay?

ARLIN. Fine.

KELLI. Drinking is a pleasure, it's not a problem.

ARLIN. I wasn't really talking about drinking.

KELLI. Well what then, because you sound perilously close to some kind of anti-drinking Al-Anon come on.

ARLIN. The loneliness.

KELLI. Oh that! That ole' thing!

(Freshening her own drink.)

Well I'll tell you, if there's anything more irritating than those straight women that come on to lesbians, it's those fucking Al-Anon Nazi Jesus Freaks and their little save-your-life sermons. At least a straight woman will quit if you say no.

ARLIN. Well, most of the time.

KELLI. But these people, these A.A. droids, won't stop unless they see you loading a shotgun!

ARLIN. I don't know who you met, but A.A. has nothing to do with preaching to people.

KELLI. Well, whatever. They just wanna get in your pants with their little do-gooder vibe.

ARLIN. That's lovely.

KELLI. No but you know what I mean, Jesus, you must be surrounded by 'em all the time, do you natter to one another about changing your lives?

ARLIN. Actually, there's a rule against talking about what goes on in meetings.

KELLI. Yes, that's what I mean! Rules! And steps & guidelines

& buddies & prayers! Isn't it just a little Christian club-housey? I see your look, Arlin, I'm not blind, you think I doth protest too much, but I'm sorry, life is not a little club-house meeting where all you have to do is follow the golden rules and say the magic pledge and everything will be sweet & sober! It's not! I'm sorry if it insults your club soda manifesto, but let's grow up & join the real world, okay? Life's hard, we live, we die, we catch a few movies. Some drink, some smoke, some peel the wall paper slowly down the wall with their teeth, whatever! Let's just not pretend it's simpler than it is. Hello, goodbye, life cannot be reduced to 12 easy steps.

ARLIN. None of them are easy.

KELLI. Oh you know what I mean! God, you're so *offendable*!

ARLIN. None of them are easy!

KELLI. Fine! The 12 *hard* steps then! You can't reduce life to 12 steps of any kind! Well, maybe you can, but I don't think they're steps like "Go apologize to everybody you ever offended!"

ARLIN. It's not –

KELLI. They'd be more like, "Go back and *live with* the people you offended." Or this, "Seek & locate the worst shit-head you were ever involved with. Marry him." That's a hard step! Now that's sobering!

ARLIN. That's *not* sobering, that'll keep you drinking forever.

KELLI. Are you speaking from personal experience?

ARLIN. Are you?

KELLI. Oo, you're getting quicker.

ARLIN. Well, I'm tired of pecking the eyes out of my values. I thought we'd switch and chew on the carnage of your life for a while.

KELLI. There's so little that hasn't been chewed already.

ARLIN. Do you have any pretzels?

KELLI. I thought you weren't staying.

ARLIN. I'm not, I just thought we'd be at dinner by now and I haven't eaten.

KELLI. I have fritos.

ARLIN. Thank you.

(KELLI *gets them.*)

I'm not staying, I just need something to bring my blood sugar up, while we're chatting with the perfectly nice alcoholic lesbian.

(KELLI *laughs.*)

KELLI. *(Off)* God, I'm so rude! Did I really say that?

ARLIN. You're actually one of the rudest people I've ever met.

KELLI. Get out!

ARLIN. Yeah, you are.

KELLI. Oh come on, some of those big, butchy gay women? They don't have mouths?

ARLIN. Dykes?

KELLI. Yeah.

ARLIN. You're allowed to say it.

KELLI. Am I? You can never tell.

ARLIN. Just be respectful.

KELLI. You're saying I'm ruder than a dyke?

ARLIN. You're much ruder than the dykes I know.

KELLI. Is that appropriate, do you think? Found some dip.

(*SHE brings food, THEY eat.*)

ARLIN. Mm, thank you. Socially, no it's not appropriate for you to be rude. Historically speaking, however, the common majority has always enjoyed the liberty of exploiting their minorities.

KELLI. What do you, teach?

ARLIN. No, but you asked.

KELLI. I'm not exploiting you.

ARLIN. You said yourself, you ask me questions you wouldn't dare to ask other people. You demand to know if I'm alcoholic, and then spend the rest of the time drinking, defending drinking and poking holes in non-drinking. And you ask personal questions about my sex life but reveal none of your own.

KELLI. I'm just curious.

ARLIN. Well maybe I'm curious too.

KELLI. I've never had sex in a bathroom, okay? I've never even had a one-night stand. There, does that make us even?

ARLIN. Why haven't you?

KELLI. *(Laughs.)* I was being careful.

ARLIN. Well, in this day & age that's good.

KELLI. It wasn't for health & safety. Jesus! I really thought that it was worth saving myself for a stable, long-term relationship.

ARLIN. Nothin' wrong with that.

KELLI. I don't know. You can go so far in any one direction doing the right thing that it somehow turns into a wrong thing. You ever have that happen? I felt morally superior for years when I fended guys off. But in the end, all it added up to was I didn't know shit about sex or men.

ARLIN. Well, sleeping around doesn't necessarily enlighten you about either one.

KELLI. Yeah?

ARLIN. Well, maybe a little the sex.

KELLI. Great.

ARLIN. I think you just have to try to be there when you're there. Doesn't mean anything to have a lot of sex if you're not home inside yourself anyway. You did it, but you missed it. Same with holding out. If you wanted to but you didn't, you're still not there. Inside, where your real self lives.

KELLI. God, is that ever true. I bet you're a good lover.

ARLIN. That actually is a line that a straight woman used to come on to me.

KELLI. Get outta here! You liar!

ARLIN. No, it is! That's exactly what she said.

KELLI. Well I'm not coming on to you! Believe me, you'd know it if I was coming on to you. I can walk into a bar and pick up a guy without ever having to say –

ARLIN. Okay shuttup.

KELLI. Only with me, he wouldn't be going anywhere or doing anything.

ARLIN. No? Are you sure?

KELLI. Yeah. I have Herpes.

ARLIN. *(Choking on a frito)* Oh. Wow.

KELLI. Flare up. All the medications seem to give me hives.

ARLIN. Ah.

KELLI. Just a little gift from one of those stable, long-term relationships.

ARLIN. Right.

KELLI. The gift that keeps on giving.

ARLIN. To you and everyone else.

KELLI. Have I embarrassed you?

ARLIN. Uh-huh.

KELLI. Good.

ARLIN. Why?

KELLI. I dunnow.

(KELLI goes back to the bar.)

ARLIN. Goin' a little fast on the flares there, aren't we, Gertie?

KELLI. Hm? Relax, I just like to keep it topped off. I haven't had four *entire* scotches, I would be on my ear. I just like the feeling of a full glass. Half a glass is wretched. It's like socks that are always falling half way down, or not having enough money for the *good* coat, only the cheap one. It's depressing. I like things full. And good. And neat.

ARLIN. Well, that's an impressive credo.

KELLI. Can I ask you something?

ARLIN. Oh God take me now.

KELLI. C'mon, you're eating my fritos.

ARLIN. So not worth it.

KELLI. You really haven't had sex in longer than me?

ARLIN. Which details you do & don't retain is very annoying.

KELLI. C'mon, I told you about my flare-up.

ARLIN. I'm sorry you have an S.T.D., it doesn't entitle you to the pitfalls of my love life.

KELLI. S.T.D.?

ARLIN. Sexually Transmitted…

KELLI. Okay, I get it, thank you. You want more drink?

ARLIN. No, thank you, I need to use the restroom.

KELLI. Door number one, pass go, collect $200.

*(**ARLIN** goes in bathroom. **KELLI** talks to her through the door.)*

So, I take it I don't get an answer, huh?

*(**KELLI** knocks)*

Arlin?

ARLIN. *(Off)* I can't talk right now, I'll be out in a minute!

KELLI. *(Knocking again.)* Then will you tell me?

ARLIN. If you don't let me pee my bladder's gonna explode!

KELLI. Gross.

(Continues to talk to her in bathroom.)

Well, that's okay. None of my business anyway, right? And it doesn't really matter whether you've had someone more recently than me or not. Wouldn't be hard. You could've made love with somebody two *seasons* ago and it would still have me beat. It's just…it would be comforting to know. Because you start to feel like you're the only celibate person on earth. Well, not exactly celibate but…singular.

(No longer necessarily to Arlin)

And meantime everybody else is having sex in *droves!*
Even women who say they aren't, the very next week-
end they meet some cute guy and sleep with him, and
then they turn out to have the most grotesquely joyous
fling! And next thing you know they're getting married in a pastel colors theme, and everybody's really
excited, because she waited *so* long for the right guy
and it's *so* great! Only the happy couple don't know
whether to invite you, because they can't remember if
they were originally your friend or Rick's. And if they
invite Rick, can they invite you too, do you & Rick get
along now, or is it just possible that you still want to *cut
off his dick a dull scissors!*

(**ARLIN** *comes out of bathroom.*)

ARLIN. What?

KELLI. Suffice it to say, I am not attracting quite the same
dating scene I did before.

ARLIN. Before what?

KELLI. Before… they redrew the Mason-Dixon line.

ARLIN. What?

KELLI. Before they redrew the map. The everything map.
Before you found out some people will put the equa-
tor any fucking place they please.

ARLIN. Um…

KELLI. Before you have any idea that this kind of thing can
happen. Before that time, you live in, whatsit, ignorant
bliss! Before the *mail* comes in, Arlin. Before the mail
comes in. *That's* where I went wrong! If anybody ever
leaves you, *don't open the mail*! It was 'Before,' before I
opened the mail! After that, it was nothing but 'After.'
Woman, Before & After, and I became the 'After'
picture.

ARLIN. You know, I think Mr. Johnnie Walker is beginning to –

KELLI. Once you open the mail, you can never go back to
ignorant bliss. Once you see the statement, you can
never go back and *not* know what it looks like when

someone has maxed out your credit cards. And you never want to know that your bank accounts can read sudden zero. You can never *not* know what a warrant looks like – it's exciting at first, even if it's not your name on it – but still, you can no longer *not* know. And anything, anything, Arlin – !

ARLIN. Yes.

KELLI. – From the I.R.S., do *not* open it, now or ever, we should all know this by now, there is *not* good news there! Why do we not learn! We open the mail and then we're an 'After' picture. And 'Before' gals are much nicer dates.

ARLIN. I expect so.

(Pause.)

KELLI. Shocked?

ARLIN. You know, I just, I went to the bathroom and kinda fell outta the loop.

KELLI. Well, keep your finances separate, Arlin, that's all I can say. If you're gonna get married, don't combine.

ARLIN. Not likely to be a problem.

KELLI. Keep everything separate! Bank accounts, charge cards, loans, taxes, credit ratings, legal charges – even if it's more costly.

ARLIN. Okay.

KELLI. Because once you're legally bonded, I think maybe love becomes irrelevant, Arlin.

ARLIN. Mm.

KELLI. If I were you, and I had it to do all over again, I'd do it like *you* did: just play the field! Go around and have *lots* of sex, no strings, just do it right there in the bathroom!

ARLIN. Well that's not –

KELLI. But don't get married, because it completely changes the definition of the phrase "getting screwed"!

(KELLI goes into a corner for a moment.)

ARLIN. I'm sorry.

KELLI. Oh, don't be nice about this.

ARLIN. I see you're still very, very hurt.

KELLI. Ach! You don't even know me.

(Pause.)

So! Did you carve your initials on the wall afterwards, or anything to mark the occasion?

ARLIN. Huh?

KELLI. Have cigarettes and flush the toilet?

ARLIN. You know, I told you about that in a passing moment. It's not a proud memory for me.

KELLI. Well, it is at least a dubious achievement!

ARLIN. It was the callous act of a drunk!

KELLI. Well, it was fun!

ARLIN. No, Kelli, it was not! It was the desperate act of somebody too fucked up to care about the consequences of their actions! Just frantically filling the moments & stuffing the silence full of noise so as never to have to feel your own pain! Billie Jean King said, "Never mistake motion for action," well that was motion, mindless and fucked-up, and really, really stupid. Not that different from the asshole who ripped you off. And it would take an asshole to prefer your money to a life with you. But that's the way it is when you're a drunken asshole. No, not even drunk, that's the way it is when you're afraid to come home to yourself because you might find that horrible emptiness waiting.

*(**KELLI** goes to refill her glass, cavalier.)*

KELLI. Hey, try coming home and finding all your furniture repossessed, now *that's* a horrible emptiness!

ARLIN. They say in A.A. not to bother bandying words with a drunk, because only one of you will remember it in the morning.

KELLI. That me? The drunk?

ARLIN. That's number six you're goin' for.

KELLI. I thought you're weren't allowed to tell your A.A. club secrets.

ARLIN. You're really hard to talk to honestly!

KELLI. Lie more.

ARLIN. I didn't come this far to live like that.

KELLI. How far have you come, Arlin? Too far & high above everybody else to lie down with us dogs? Do everyone a favor, make a mess!

ARLIN. I'm not gonna get baited into this.

KELLI. Slum with us once in a while, it would do a lot for your entertainment value, frankly, particularly as a date!

(**ARLIN** *puts on her coat.*)

ARLIN. Well, that's all of this bullshit I'm up to.

KELLI. That's fine. Because the sheen coming off your A.A. tiara is giving me a migraine.

ARLIN. What is it with you and A.A.?! You're so bitter, did somebody try an intervention on you or something?

KELLI. Man, I thought you were going!

ARLIN. I am, Jesus Christ, and thanks for a lovely evening!

(**ARLIN** *holds out her glass to* **KELLI**, *who doesn't take it.*)

KELLI. Puh! If that's all the heat you can take on your straight & narrow path – well, narrow anyway – no wonder you're desperate for a date on Friday night!

(**KELLI** *walks out of the room.*

ARLIN *hurls the glass against a wall, it shatters. Her head jerks back, struck by flying glass.*)

ARLIN. Oh!

(**KELLI** *comes back.*)

KELLI. What the fuck are you doing?!

ARLIN. God!

(*SHE moves to Arlin.*)

KELLI. Are you hurt?

ARLIN. Yes.

KELLI. Lemme see.

ARLIN. *(Turning away)* No.

KELLI. Alright, I'm gonna get you a cloth. Siddown.

*(**KELLI** gets a cloth from the bar area.)*

ARLIN. A piece of glass ricocheted.

KELLI. That's what you get.

(Bringing a cloth.)

Here, lemme see.

ARLIN. I can do it.

KELLI. Fine.

*(**KELLI** slips on her shoes, starts to pick up shards of glass.)*

When I said, "Do us a favor, make a mess," I didn't mean in my house tonight.

*(**ARLIN** comes over, nursing her face.)*

ARLIN. Did I get blood on your floor?

KELLI. A little with the glass, it'll come up.

ARLIN. Lemme do it.

KELLI. Don't worry about it, go wash your face.

ARLIN. You should use rubber gloves.

KELLI. It's not a problem.

ARLIN. If that's my blood, you should use rubber gloves.

KELLI. Well why, it's not like you have…

*(**KELLI** stops.*

ARLIN *watches her response warily.*

It hits **KELLI** *hard, this reality. That Arlin's blood is not safe. What that means.*

THEY stand staring at one another, emotions running beneath frozen exteriors. Finally **ARLIN** *moves.)*

ARLIN. As a precaution. Use some gloves.

KELLI. *(Softly)* Okay.

> (**ARLIN** *goes OFF into bathroom.*
>
> **KELLI** *goes OFF into kitchen, comes back wearing rubber gloves, cleans up, still shaken.*)

ARLIN. *(Off)* You have Band-Aids?

KELLI. In the medicine cabinet, in a pink thing.

> *(Pause.)*

Find one?

> (**ARLIN** *emerges with one. SHE sits on the couch, putting the Band-Aid on her own face.*
>
> *The air is heavy between THEM, with their previous angry words, and this new fact. THEY take refuge in their small tasks.*)

ARLIN. Sorry about your glass.

KELLI. I hated that glass anyway.

ARLIN. Oh yeah, it was a really horrible glass.

> *(An awkward silence.*
>
> **ARLIN** *rises.*)

Well. At the risk of being redundant, I really do think it's time for me to go.

KELLI. You missed.

ARLIN. Hm?

> (**KELLI** *points to Arlin's Band-Aid.*)

Oh.

> (**ARLIN** *adjusts the Band-Aid on her cheek.*)

Okay?

KELLI. Not quite.

> (**ARLIN** *pulls the Band-Aid off and re-sticks it.*)

ARLIN. I get it?

KELLI. Well… you…

> *(Hesitantly, **KELLI** reaches up and tries to fix it, but it's*

tricky with rubber gloves on.)

It's uh...Here.

(**KELLI** *pulls her gloves off and adjusts the bandage. It's lost its adhesive.)*

This one's all screwed up. You're gonna have to start over.

(**ARLIN** *reaches for the used Band-Aid.)*

It's not gonna kill me.

(**ARLIN** *goes into the bathroom.*

KELLI *throws the old bandage away.*

ARLIN *emerges opening a new one.*

KELLI *takes it from her.)*

Okay, you're gonna mess this up again. Sit.

(**ARLIN** *sits.)*

Now, this is not a come-on.

(*SHE sits beside* **ARLIN**, *puts the Band-Aid on her, sticking its edges to Arlin's face carefully, tenderly.*

SHE traces the outline of the Band-Aid, touches Arlin's face. **ARLIN** *closes her eyes.* **KELLI** *holds Arlin's face in her hand. Not so much sexually as intimately, with the knowledge of Arlin's mortality hanging over them, and loneliness hovering around them, and all that has passed between them. A long moment.*

THEY break apart simultaneously.)

KELLI. Well...

ARLIN. Yeah.

KELLI. I think I'm gonna...

(*SHE is already making a beeline for the bar, but veers off.)*

Fuck. What am I supposed to do with myself if I'm not gonna come over here & get a drink every five minutes?

ARLIN. I dunnow.

KELLI. It's very convenient, for those in between moments...
like now.

ARLIN. Drink seltzer.

KELLI. You drank it all. Bubble junkie.

(The conversation beaches again.)

ARLIN. Hey c'mon, don't get all shy on me now, dudette.
You've shouted at me & thrown me out, don't get all
weird now just because I bled in your house.

KELLI. I'm not.

ARLIN. I'm kidding.

KELLI. I know.

ARLIN. Quoting *you.*

KELLI. I'm so rude.

ARLIN. Ruder than dykes. Tell all your friends.

*(**KELLI** looks around. A sad silence, but genuine.)*

KELLI. It doesn't make me uncomfortable.

ARLIN. Good.

KELLI. It makes me sad. It makes me really, really sad,
Arlin.

ARLIN. Yeah. You have a nice apartment by the way. What
do you do?

KELLI. Computer systems analysis. For a small company. I
don't feel good.

ARLIN. I know. I wish I could say you'll feel better soon, but
I think with you, it's gonna get harder before it gets
easier.

KELLI. Why?

ARLIN. Because I don't think you're used to having your
feelings. You're stubborn. And you're on the verge.

KELLI. Fuck. And what about you, you just have it all
together?

ARLIN. *(Laughs.)* Yeah. Right.

KELLI. I'm sorry.

ARLIN. For what?

KELLI. The things I said earlier.

ARLIN. Because I have HIV?

KELLI. No. Because it was rude.

ARLIN. So you admit you're rude.

KELLI. I already said I was rude.

ARLIN. Ruder thaaan…

KELLI. Dykes. Big, big dykes. Much ruder.

ARLIN. Well okay. Now all we need is to get you a tattoo & a buzz cut & a big Harley.

KELLI. You're so fucked up.

ARLIN. I get scared sometimes. Because I feel my mortality closer than most women my age. And I'm lonely a lot of the time. I dunno, I think it's just the phase I'm in. But mostly, I wouldn't trade it, Kelli. Not even to have all my health back, I wouldn't. I wouldn't go back where you are now, you're a friend but I have to say that. And it's not that you can't do it, and it's not that I don't have any pain. But I'm home. I'm in here. I'm lookin' out of my eyes. And it counts. I mean, some mornings something as simple as a glass of water just *sends* me! And then some mornings I wake up mad as hell, and y'know what? That's a good thing too.

Because most of my life I felt too not-worth-it to risk upsetting anybody or taking anybody's time or, heaven forbid, letting some of that rage out because there was so much of it, if it ever started it would drown the world! So I would just *eat*!

And Jesus, is it any wonder so many women have weight issues? We're raised as second class citizens until we're up to *here* with it, but by that time our self esteem is down to *here*! So between here & here we just become *inert*! Sorry, I'm off on a diatribe.

KELLI. That's okay, go ahead, live it up. Today only, no charge.

(**ARLIN** *rises, too delectable an invitation to resist.*)

ARLIN. Well, alright then, lemme do it right!

(SHE stands, enjoying it for once.)

The word Mankind, as in the species Man: gotta go! On the wall at the planetarium it says, "A man can reach the stars if he can dream of it!" And I want to say, for my little 9-year-old niece, "What about women?" And they say, "Oh, well, by Man we mean everyone, all Mankind!" But I don't think my niece thinks of herself as Mankind, I think she just feels left out. But hey, when you run the language, you call the shots. Who decided we were *Man*kind? It's not our story, it's *his*tory! And it's all like that, it's all male-oriented, even God! And it *sounds* like small stuff, but it's subtle, like HIV. Once it gets in the blood, it effects everything. Except one word. I know one female-rooted word! You know what it is?

KELLI. What?

ARLIN. Commence. Co-mensing, as in menstruation? To mense together. Let us commence. Meaning to flow forward together. Isn't that nice?

KELLI. *Nice*?! Something in your diatribe is actually nice?

ARLIN. Yeah. One thing. It's a start. Let us commence. Put that in your computer systems analysis.

KELLI. Hey, don't knock it, it's a good gig.

ARLIN. Knock.

KELLI. Well, what do you do, smarty-pants?

ARLIN. Uummm… kinda rather not say.

KELLI. Something is seriously wrong with the world when people will tell you where they've had sex but not what they do for a living.

ARLIN. I make deliveries.

KELLI. Well, that's alright, that's a respectable job. Unless it's something illegal.

ARLIN. No. *(Muttering)* I deliver flhs.

KELLI. What?

ARLIN. I deliver flowers.

KELLI. Get outta here! You do not!

ARLIN. I do, I work for a florist.

KELLI. Well no wonder I thought you were the flower delivery person, you *are* the flower delivery person!!

ARLIN. So what?

KELLI. So you were delivering flowers! So I was right! Intuitively I was right!

ARLIN. So?

KELLI. So, you were so pissed off & righteous! And you really *were* the flower delivery person!

ARLIN. No I wasn't, I was your date.

KELLI. And you probably got the flowers for free.

ARLIN. No. Half price.

KELLI. God, 60 bucks, and you threw 'em all over the floor.

ARLIN. Well, I was upset, my date was a bust.

KELLI. No it wasn't. It wasn't even a date.

ARLIN. No? What was it?

> (**KELLI** *goes to the stereo, flips on MUSIC, the same song as the top of the show.*
>
> *SHE turns it up and starts to dance.*)

KELLI. It was a commencement!

> (*THEY laugh.* **ARLIN** *watches* **KELLI,** *bashful. But, what the hell, it is a great song.* **KELLI** *and* **ARLIN** *dance around the apartment with growing abandon.*
>
> *LIGHTS FADE as MUSIC grows.*)

PROP LIST

1 Bouquet of flowers
Kelli's wallet
A $10 bill
A $20 bill
Phone
Kelli's 'date coat'
1 Glass for drinking club soda
1 Whiskey glass
1 Breakaway glass
1 Bottle of Johnny Walker scotch
1 Ice bucket
1 Bowl of Frito's
1 Bar towel or tea towel
Boom and dustpan
1 Pair of rubber gloves
2 Band-Aids

FRIENDS OF THE DECEASED

Vanessa Shealy and Pamela Dunlap at Vital Theatre

SETTING

A fresh grave in a cemetery. No headstone, a few folding chairs.

TIME

10 minutes.

ROLES

VI – An older woman. Wealthy, sophisticated, wit of acid.
LANIE – A teen. Street savvy and naiveté. A runaway.

*(**AT RISE:** A soft THUNDER as lights come up on a completed funeral. Some folding chairs, a fresh grave.*

VI, *an older woman in an elegant raincoat, sits a distance from it.*

LANIE, *a grungy young woman with no raincoat & a small BACK-PACK, enters without seeing* **VI** *and comes to the grave. SHE stands looking at it a long moment.)*

VI. Were you a friend of the deceased?

LANIE. What?

VI. I'm sorry, I've interrupted you.

LANIE. No, that's okay. I was just, y'know, staring.

VI. Were you a friend of the deceased?

LANIE. You know what? No.

VI. Oh. Are you related?

LANIE. No. Are you?

VI. I'm his wife.

LANIE. Oh, it's a him.

VI. Yes. You don't know him at all?

LANIE. Huh-uh.

VI. Do you mind if I ask what you're doing here?

LANIE. Mourning, geez, state the obvious. You?

VI. He's my husband.

LANIE. I know, but like, why are you here now?

VI. It's his funeral. And if you didn't know Gerald –

LANIE. But the funeral was over two & a half hours ago.

VI. Were you waiting for me to leave?

LANIE. I mean, I know he's your husband & all, but I waited in the rain a long time, I thought it was my turn.

VI. How can you mourn if you don't even know him?

LANIE. I'm a sad person. What about you?

VI. He was my husband.

LANIE. Right, you said that.

VI. I have a right to be here.

LANIE. Everybody has a right to mourn.

VI. This is my husband's funeral and if you didn't know Gerald then you should leave.

LANIE. Everybody else is gone, y'know.

VI. This is a very personal matter.

LANIE. Yeah, no shit, it's personal to me too, okay?

VI. Why!

LANIE. Hey, I have feelings too, ya know, it's a funeral, I'm grieving!

(**VI** *puts her head in her hands.*)

Oh, shit…um…We're both sad, okay?

VI. Oh, I just hate him!

LANIE. Whoa. Look, I really thought you were through.

VI. I will never be through!

LANIE. You just said you hated him.

VI. You are extremely impertinent!

LANIE. Look, if I knew you were still with Gerald I'd of waited.

VI. So you do know him.

LANIE. No.

VI. You knew his name.

LANIE. You just said it.

VI. You're one of them, aren't you?

LANIE. Who?

VI. Don't play sweet & low with me, dear. I knew all about it. There were others you know.

LANIE. Other mourners?

VI. Other chicks. "A twat for every city" was how I think he phrased it, in one of his lesser moments.

LANIE. Gross.

VI. So don't think you're special.

LANIE. I wasn't his chick, okay?

VI. What then? Masseuse? Fuck-buddy? Whatever, the free ride's over. Unless you want to dig him up. No doubt he's still *stiff.*

LANIE. Ew!

VI. Yes, thank you, Viagra. If you hear a knocking on the box, it's not his hand.

LANIE. You are, like, major in the bitterness department.

VI. Yes well, it was a bitter pill.

LANIE. That is sad.

VI. If sorrow burned calories, dear, we'd all be supermodels.

LANIE. I'll find another funeral.

VI. No, by all means, stay. I have so much bitterness to share. Who better to stick it to?

LANIE. How 'bout your husband? He's the one who couldn't keep his pecker packed.

VI. I just wanted to see who he unpacked for.

LANIE. Well now you've seen me, and spread your toxic vibes all over me, so are we done?

VI. Oh, I'm just starting. In fact, when I'm done with you, do you know what I think I'll do?

LANIE. Have yourself committed?

VI. I'm going to track you all down, one by one.

LANIE. Okay, this is why I prefer the dead. The living are way scarier.

(**LANIE** *picks up her PACK to go.*

VI *takes a FAT PACKET OF MONEY from her purse and tosses it down.*

LANIE *stops.*)

…What is that?

VI. What's your name?

LANIE. Lanie.

VI. Well, Lanie, it's for you.

LANIE. Is it real?

VI. All hundreds.

LANIE. Wow.…Why?

VI. Because he would have hated it. I was going to give it to Greenpeace. He just loathed liberals. But I think this is better. Casting his life savings to the chippies.

LANIE. Well, it's not like I couldn't use it. I have, like, no money.

(VI *tosses a 2nd PACKET OF MONEY at her feet.*)

Are you totally rich or what?!

VI. I call it Condom Money. Every trip, he made another wad & met another slut.

LANIE. Um, look, I really didn't know him.

(VI *tosses out a 3rd PACKET of money.*)

VI. Yes you did.

LANIE. What, you want me to lie?

(*Throws down a 4th PACKET.*)

VI. Yes.

LANIE. Sheezus!

VI. $100,000. That ought to buy a confession.

LANIE. This is heavy.

VI. I abhor your vocabulary. 12 years of public school and you choose to talk like pseudo nouveau hippie trash.

LANIE. Nice.

VI. And your little bare midriff. I've always wanted to tell you girls how apt it is that you should tattoo yourselves. They did the same to whores in the 1600's.

LANIE. If I cared about an old bag's opinion, I'd go to a recycling bin.

VI. Do you want the money or not? Yes, you do. So, no hitting back. This is my game. *My* dalliance. Sit down.

(**LANIE** *hesitates.* **VI** *puts the MONEY by a chair.* **LANIE** *sits.*)

Now, three questions. What kind of sex did you have?

LANIE. This is sick.

VI. Humor me, you can afford it. What kind of sex?

*(**LANIE** shifts uncomfortably.)*

LANIE. Um...Oral.

VI. On him or you?

LANIE. Uh...

VI. It's usually on the man.

LANIE. Him.

VI. Did he come in your mouth?

*(**LANIE** squirms.)*

Alright, it doesn't matter, next question. Did he use a condom?

LANIE. Yes. Always. Lots of 'em.

VI. How enchanting.

LANIE. That's three questions.

VI. That was the initial interview. Now the specifics.

LANIE. Forget it.

VI. Did he say he loved you?

*(**LANIE** starts to get up. **VI** puts the MONEY in her hands.)*

Hold onto this, you're almost there.

LANIE. Like this is really gonna make you feel better.

VI. I'm not looking to feel better. Answer the question.

LANIE. I dunnow wh –

VI. Make it up!

LANIE. But I didn –

VI. Look, you're the same age, you've got the look, it doesn't matter whether it was you or not! You're all the same to me. I need to hear it.

LANIE. Why?

VI. I'm enraged.

LANIE. Yeah, let's reinforce that.

VI. I want to hear every obscene word and repulsive act, every seedy little detail down to the tits, until anything I feel for him is utterly obliterated!

LANIE. I don't think it works that way.

VI. Did he say he loved you!

LANIE. Sheezus! This is worse than waitressing!

VI. Please.

LANIE. *(A gentler approach)* Okay…No. He said he cared for me but he couldn't really love anyone other than his wife.

*(**VI** is silent a moment.)*

VI. That was tricky.

LANIE. Well, it's possible.

VI. No it's not! You're just a stand-in, play the role right!

LANIE. I can't!

VI. He fucked his way across the map! Don't tell me he cared for either one of us!

LANIE. Well, fucking isn't everything! It doesn't mean you don't count, as a person!

VI. You were an extra to him. A prop! One doesn't care what happens to the props once the show is over. You were disposable!…As was I.

LANIE. This sucks.

VI. He once asked me if he could tie me down and perform cunnilingus. I told him not unless he wanted to be a necrophiliac too. Did you know sarcasm can kill a relationship? The young can get away with it, but don't use it when you're married. By then it's just pain with a punch-line. Talk to one another if you can. Your generation has a better chance than we did. You have that whole feeling thing.

LANIE. You don't have feelings?

VI. A variation on Darwin, Survival of the Numbest. So, when you were in bed together, did he ask such things of you?

LANIE. I dunnow. I don't even know what you said, what's a neropholiac?

VI. Never mind, don't invent, just draw from experience.

LANIE. I can't....I don't have any.

VI. You have no experience with boys?

LANIE. No.

VI. Girls?

(**LANIE** *scowls.*)

You're telling me you're a virgin? But you're so... sleazy.

LANIE. This is the how girls dress now! Where've you been, in a cellar?

VI. Do you all let your hair get so greasy?

LANIE. No! I haven't had a chance to shower in a while!

(**VI** *packs up the money.*)

VI. Well, I can't do this with a virgin.

LANIE. Wait a minute, I answered your questions!

VI. Sorry.

LANIE. Then gimmie another chance! I can do better! Really! Please. I really need the money. Try me.

(**VI** *hesitates.*)

...Just tell me how much you want it to hurt.

VI. Enough to finish him off completely.

LANIE. Okay. Fine. Shitty, painful & bitter, right?

VI. Look, I mistook you for a woman.

LANIE. And I mistook you for a human!

(**LANIE** *points to a chair.*)

You can have your money back if you're not satisfied.

(**VI** *sits.* **LANIE** *paces, tossing the story out.*)

Okay. I was this total freak at home, right? So I ran away a couple weeks ago. And I hitchhiked all the way here. And couple nights ago, this guy stopped & offered me a ride. He seemed really nice. And it was Gerald.

VI. Really.

LANIE. Really. He's a really nice guy, right? He even bought me some McDonald's. And I was thinkin', wow, this is gonna work out, I'm gonna do okay. And then when we got here, instead of dropping me at my friend's, he pulls over in this, like, warehouse parking lot –

(VI starts to get up.)

VI. That is not something Gerald would –

LANIE. Hey! *I'm* telling the story now!…

(VI sits.)

LANIE. So of course he asks if he can feel me up. And, I was so stupid, I thought if I just talked to him like a person, he would understand, 'cause he's this really nice guy, y'know? So I tell him, like, I'm not into that, that I'm saving myself for marriage. And it was like I set off a bomb, he just turns into this total freak right in the car! And he started –

VI. I really don't care to –

LANIE. – No, you'll like this, this is the painful part! He started grabbing me all over me and he got over on my side of the car and…then he…he…hurt me.

(LANIE stares off. Uncomfortable silence.)

VI. That is not a good story.

LANIE. Right. That's what makes it so perfect. You want details?

VI. No.

LANIE. Then I'll just finish…. Afterwards he let me out of the car and left me there. But it was like, part of me never got out of the car. I don't think he meant to. But he drove off with this murdered kid. And I just didn't know that could happen. That a part of you could die.…Maybe later he left her by a dumpster. And somebody found the body and took it to a morgue. They never will know who she was. So they buried her in an unmarked grave. The dirt is still fresh.

(SHE looks at the grave.)

So I came to mourn her.

*(Silence. **VI** shifts, uncomfortable with the moment and utterly at a loss what to do with it.)*

VI. Well.

*(**LANIE** stirs, tries for bravado.)*

LANIE. Horrible enough for you?

VI. Yes.

LANIE. Told you I'd make it a good one.

(SHE moves a distance off, trying to recover herself.

VI stands, looks around uncertainly. Finally SHE picks up the MONEY.)

VI. Here.

*(**LANIE** regards it blankly.)*

LANIE. Nah.

VI. You should take it. Really.

*(**LANIE** shakes her head.)*

We had an agreement. I won't have it said I welch on a deal.

*(**LANIE** doesn't.)*

Go on. Take it. I would like you to have it.

*(Tries to put the money in **LANIE**'s limp hands.)*

For heaven's sake, you said you needed money, go on and have it! Take it! What is wrong with you!

*(**LANIE** moves away.)*

What is it you want?! That's all I can do! I can't…

*(**VI** finally stops, the money drooping in her hands.)*

This is what I have. I have money. I don't have anything else.

LANIE. Then part of you is lost too.

VI. All of me is lost.

LANIE. You still feel things.

VI. Yes.

LANIE. Well, that's a good sign.

VI. I find it extremely painful.

*(**LANIE** goes to the grave.)*

LANIE. It's a funeral, it should be.

VI. I will never not miss him.

LANIE. I know.

VI. I have no idea how to go on.

*(**VI** stands emptily. **LANIE** just stares at the grave.)*

Please let me help you.

LANIE. Mourn with me.

VI. Does it do any good?

LANIE. You can't go on if you don't, y'know, mourn the you that's gone.

*(**VI** watches her.)*

VI. Will it end?

LANIE. The mourning? I dunnow.

*(**VI** finally walks down and takes a place beside her. THEY look at the grave a long moment.)*

Were you a friend of the deceased?

VI. I was, a long time ago. I let her slip away.

LANIE. Mine was instant. It's really sad.…

(A soft, distant THUNDER.)

LANIE. She would have been a lovely young woman.

VI. Yes. She is.

(LIGHTS FADE on THEM together.)

PROPS

Vi's Purse
Lanie's Backpack
4 Packets of money

THE LAST NICKEL

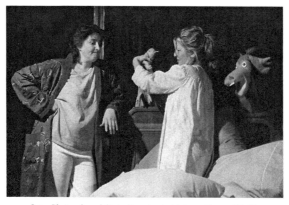

*Jane Shepard and Kate Bennis, puppeteers George Sheffey
and Jack Nagle, at One Dream Theatre*

SET

Jamie's bedroom, night.
Bed with backboard, chair, bedside table, lamp.

TIME

40 minutes.

ROLES

JAMIE – A woman
JO – Her younger sister
2 Puppeteers:
1 – Moose / Nurse 1
2 – Tim / Dave / Nurse 2

(SETTING: JAMIE's bedroom, night, lights dim.

AT RISE: JAMIE is asleep in bed. JO appears at the doorway.)

JO. Jamie.

(No response.)

Woo-hoo.

(Nothing.)

Jamie, wake up. The house is on fire.

(JAMIE sleeps on.)

I'm taking all your possessions and moving to Pennsylvania.

(Nothing. JO comes to bed.)

Sssssst. Jamie, your bladder is full. If you don't wake up now you're gonna wet the bed.

(Makes NOISES: raspberries, farts, whatever might work.)

Oh, poop.

(Jumps on bed, singing.)

"I'm a little tea pot short & stout,

Here is my handle, here is my spout.

When I get all steamed up, hear me shout… "

(JAMIE simply turns over.)

Tsk.

(JO gives up, goes to the door, lingers a moment, EXITS.

Silence.

JO ENTERS with TROMBONE.)

"Ode to Jamie."

(SHE PLAYS loudly. **JAMIE** *jumps, snapping on bedside lamp.)*

JAMIE. Alright alright alright, stop it! Jo!

*(***JO*** *stops.)*

It's Tuesday. I have to work tomorrow. I'm not doing this tonight.

*(***JO*** *toots.)*

Jo!

*(***JO*** *lowers the trombone.* **JAMIE** *punches her pillow.)*

That's stupid, you don't even play the trombone.

JO. But it's cute! Don'tcha think it's a neat image? I could make it all the rage! Arr, the trombone pirate!

JAMIE. Did you hear me?

JO. Do you think a tuba would be funnier? Just the word: "tuba." Plosives are funny.

JAMIE. I'm not doing this.

JO. "Tuba," tell me you don't think that's funny.

JAMIE. It's not.

JO. Anything with P's or T's. Poodle. Tu-tu poodles.

JAMIE. Don't.

JO. Pee-pee?

JAMIE. Jo…

JO. Pee-pee poodles!

JAMIE. God!

JO. Puppy! No poo-poo in tuba!

JAMIE. We agreed you weren't going to do this anymore.

JO. You decided, technically that is not an agreement.

JAMIE. You said you wouldn't wake me up anymore.

JO. I'm lonely.

JAMIE. You just can't keep doing this to me. I need my sleep.

JO. Or lonesome. That sounds better. I'm lonesome, Jamie.

(Climbing onto bed with her.)

Calamity Jane, in her letters to her daughter, used to call it a "high lonesome." Where you go out on the high plains by yourself for some time, you just disappear, and everybody in town wonders where Calamity's got to. And she's out on the prairie by a campfire, drinkin' herself blind, and havin' trouble writin' her little Janie anymore, 'cause her ink's near used up, and her eyesight's failin'. And the last thing she ever wrote to her daughter was, "Forgive me, Janey, and consider I was lonesome."

JAMIE. *(Unmoved)* That's very interesting.

JO. Well that's me, I'm on a hiiigh lonesome.

JAMIE. I know. And I'm sorry. But I am too, kid, everybody's alone, that's the way it is. Except for a few good years here & there, when you get a brief respite, but on the whole you know as well as I do, "You are the only person – "

BOTH. " – With whom you will live your entire life."

JAMIE. Well it's true, get used to it.

(**JAMIE** *lies down again.*)

JO. Fine for you.

JAMIE. Your keeping me awake is not fair, I have to function tomorrow. Go bug somebody else.

(Pushes her off bed & turns over.)

You're a good sister, I love you, go in peace.

(**JO** *sinks down against the wall.*)

JO. (Q*uietly*) The planet Jupiter is 40 million miles away. They talk about visiting other planets, but it's *40 million miles.* If we sent someone right now, it wouldn't even *arrive* until 2,038. And for them to get back, it would take until they were 90 years old. If they ever got back at all.

(**JAMIE** *sighs loudly.*)

I'm talking quietly. And when he got there, what would he find? Signs of previous life, little bacteria fossils, but not necessarily people. We've never seen signs of anything even remotely like life. Maybe in some other galaxy, but not here. Do you know what that means?

JAMIE. It means I'm going to kill you with an axe.

JO. It means, this is it. As far as finding companionship, you can forget it. There are no neighboring party planets, we're not gonna find company any time soon. Maybe ever. We're it. The singular little island surrounded by space & vacant bodies. The only oasis with conscious life, floating around, with just enough awareness to know how alone we are. Don't you think that's scary?

(JAMIE sits up, turns on light, pulls box of CRACKERS from under bed.)

JO. Oh. Hungry?

JAMIE. Can't sleep when I'm hungry.

JO. Can't sleep anyway.

JAMIE. Pretty happy with yourself, aren't you?

JO. No, pretty bored with myself. But *you're* pretty interesting.

JAMIE. Oh here we go.

JO. You worry me.

JAMIE. Oh yeah. I'm sleeping peacefully, you're the one barging around with a trombone, ranting about Calamity Jane, you should worry about me.

JO. I'm a wone-wy Jo-Jo.

JAMIE. You're a poop-head.

JO. Yeah.

JAMIE. You're acting like a bratty little sister.

JO. Yep.

JAMIE. I love you very much.

JO. Can I get in bed?

JAMIE. No.

(JO lies on floor watching.)

JO. Wish *I* had a snack.

JAMIE. Can't help you there.

JO. Nobody loves me, everybody hates me, I'm gonna go eat worms.

(**JAMIE** *pulls a bottle of YOO-HOO chocolate drink from under the bed and drinks it off.*)

That's new.

JAMIE. Tired of being thirsty.

JO. Yeah, but that's chocolate, and chocolate has caffeine, and caffeine keeps you awake. No wonder you're up all night.

JAMIE. Funny.

JO. Wish I had a Yoo-Hoo….

(Funny voice)

"Yoo-Hoo! Where are you? Lil' chocolate Yoo-Hoo, I'm so worried about you!"

JAMIE. What do you want, Jo?

JO. Don't get all huffy-serious. If you get all huffy-serious you'll never get back to sleep.

JAMIE. I *am* gonna get back to sleep! Because I've got a damn day tomorrow. I took a sleeping pill, I had a snack, I'm not thirsty, and I deserve to rest! I did *everything* right today! I worked hard, I waited 'til I was tired, and I *was* asleep! Godammit, I have to take care of myself now, Jo! I know this is hard for you. I know you can't rest! But I can't help you. I've tried! I sit up with you, I calm you, I listen, we party, we cry, we sit in trances! It makes no difference! I am just a person. I am a mortal human being, I can't resolve this for you.

JO. You're my sister.

JAMIE. Yes, I'm not your babysitter! I'm not your anchor! I'm not your life, okay?

JO. That's really mean. I'm not trying to take over your life, I'm just having a hard time right now. Who am I supposed to turn to?

JAMIE. I don't know. God.

JO. God! God doesn't answer questions on how to deal with death. It's policy. He never answers anything directly, but, at least with other stuff you eventually figure it out. It unfolds, and you go, "Oh! That's wasn't chaos, it was a lesson! I get it now, thank you!" Or you get a sign. A flower blooms that never bloomed before, or a bird lands on you, or a Pez candy miraculously speaks! Something to indicate meaning!

JAMIE. Never mind –

JO. But ask about death… "Um, God, about death?"

(As God)

"Sh! Can't talk about it!" …

(Self)

But, God – God? Hello? Are you listening!

(God)

"What?! I gave you the 10 commandments, what more do you want!"

(Self)

Well, I honor my mother and father & I don't pray to idols, how does this help me with the death thing? –

(God)

"Look! You're just an individual, I'm omnipotent, it's busy! I don't have time to deal with every little question you have, think about it, you'll figure it out! Just think, think all the time, mull it over, carry it with you, take it to work, bring it home, stay up all night asking questions. Think 'til you're pale and you've got big rings under your eyes. Think 'til you're living on crackers and chocolate drink –

JAMIE. Get off my bed.

JO. If you think about it all the time –

JAMIE. Get off, I said!

JO. If you think about it 'til you're *living* death, and *breathing* death –

JAMIE. Now!

(**JO** *moves off the bed.*)

JO. – Then maybe you'll get it, white girl.

JAMIE. Up yours.

(**JAMIE** *shuts off the light, throws the crackers across the room, and lays down.*)

JO. Once you get completely *inside* the death thing, maybe it'll make sense. Because you'll be dead.

JAMIE. *(Coldly)* Goodnight.

JO. I just want to talk –

JAMIE. We talked. You can't deal with it and neither can I. Goodnight.

JO. I just –

JAMIE. Goodnight.

JO. I –

JAMIE. Goodnight.

JO. Well we figured that the fuck out, didn't we?

(**JO** *EXITS, closing door.*)

JAMIE. Thank you, God!

(Tries to settle herself, more genuinely)

Thank you for the quiet. Thank you for this beautiful day. Thank you for helping me to continue on. Please let her get through this, I'm asking you, for my sake and hers, just please let her shut the hell up! In your name I ask this. Um… Amen.

(She turns over. Silence.

Two small SPOT LIGHTS snap on, two children's **HAND PUPPETS** *pop up from behind her bed: A* **MOOSE** *and* **TIM***, a stupid PIG. THEY speak in big cartoony voices, like announcers in a bizarre game show. VOICES have reverb, and seem to come from everywhere.)*

MOOSE. Odd man! She said it first, Tim, ooooodd man!

TIM. *(Snorts.)*

JAMIE. Oh, no…

MOOSE. It's that time again!

TIM. *(Snorts.)*

JAMIE. No no no!

MOOSE. What's that ya say, Tim? What time *is* it?

TIM. *(Snorts a question)*

MOOSE. Iiiiit's puppet time!

TIM. *(Squeal!)*

JAMIE. I hate the puppets!

MOOSE. Time for another nightly sojourn into the land that time forgot!

> **(PUPPETS** *cheer, confetti.* **JAMIE** *rushes to door.)*

JAMIE. We're not doing the puppets! Not tonight!

MOOSE. It's time to tickle the toes of truculent tenacity! Who's on first, Tim?

JAMIE. JO!

MOOSE. No! I'm sorry, the answer is not "Jo," I'm afraid you've lost the patio set!

JAMIE. Jo, get in here!

MOOSE. It's Jamie time! And odd man to that!

JAMIE. Shit.

MOOSE. Tim, do you remember the time Jo was taught to pray in kindergarten?

TIM. *(Snorts.)*

MOOSE. It was the first time she ever prayed, remember, Tim?

TIM. *(Snorts.)*

MOOSE. And the teacher said, "Students, here is how we pray: 'Now we thank you for this food, amen'."

JAMIE. I'm not listening to this.

MOOSE. And Jo said it, but she just had to wonder, Tim, why did we say 'odd man' at the end?

TIM. *(Snorts.)*

MOOSE. So she went to ask her big sister! Jamie's almost eight so she'll know!

(**JAMIE** *pushes PUPPETS down.*)

JAMIE. Shut up and stop it, you stupid idiots!

(*THEY pop back up.*)

MOOSE. And do you remember what Jamie said, Tim? It's so cute, it's a shame it can't be bottled.

JAMIE. Jo, for God's sake!

MOOSE. "Well," says Jamie, "I don't know why we say 'odd man.' Maybe men are just odd!"

(**PUPPETS** *laugh and squeal uproariously.*

JAMIE *tries to grab them, THEY elude her.*)

JAMIE. It's not funny any more! We didn't know how to pray, so what!

(*SHE catches* **TIM** *and throws him across the room. Tim expels a snurk and expires.*

JO *is watching from doorway.*)

JO. Aw, you killed Tim.

JAMIE. I hate the puppets.

(**MOOSE** *pops up with* **DAVE**: *a BIRD puppet.*)

MOOSE. She hates that, Dave! How do you see it?

DAVE. Paul, the stress is starting to show! They're in the home stretch, but it's still anybody's game!

MOOSE. Right you are, Dave! Jamie's shown a lot of character!

DAVE. Oh, a lot of character!

MOOSE. You have to admire that! Interrupted nights, grief, guilt, the whole history thing, she's seen it all! A real family player!

DAVE. So true, Paul! But how long can she sustain it? It's been a long game and hey-ya! The opponent shows no sign of weakening!

MOOSE. From your mouth to God's ear, Dave!

DAVE. Time, time, Paul, it's just a matter of time!

(**MOOSE** *pops up with ALARM CLOCK in his mouth.*)

MOOSE. Mm-hmm!

DAVE. And how much of it can there be left?

(*ALARM goes off.*)

Oops! Time's up! Did I call that one or what!

MOOSE. (*Spitting out clock*) You called it, Dave!

(*Smacks lips.*)

And it leaves a bad taste in everyone's mouth! Commentary?

DAVE. Only this! It's time for a word from our sponsor!

(*THEY withdraw.*)

JAMIE. The bird's new.

JO. Well you killed the pig.

JAMIE. I think you made your point now.

(**PUPPETS** *reappear with BOTTLES OF YOO-HOO.*)

DAVE. Yoo-Hoo, Paul!

MOOSE. (*bottle in mouth*) Hoo-hoo, have!

JAMIE. Okay, fine, live it up.

(**JAMIE** *faces the chair away from them, sits lighting a cigarette.*)

Lemme know when you're done.

DAVE. Speaking of done, Paul!

MOOSE. Mm-hmm!

DAVE. I have a message from the great beyond!

MOOSE. Yef?

DAVE. It's a little hint about a heavenly drink!

MOOSE. Mm-hmm!

DAVE. Sometimes, don't you just wanna feel like crap, Paul?

MOOSE. Mm!

DAVE. Then yoo-hoo, friend, I have a drink for you. Enough of this will render any player incomprehensible!

MOOSE. His a hyohec hoo, have!

DAVE. What's that, Paul?

MOOSE. *(Spits out BOTTLE.)* I said, it's a diarrheic too, Dave!

JAMIE. I can sit here all night.

MOOSE. But, God's honest truth now, Dave! Y'know what really tops off that artificial non-diary beverage?

DAVE. I think I know, Paul!

(**DAVE** *pops up with a CARTON OF CIGARETTES.*)

About a million big ol' cancer sticks! Cuts down on all that pesky breathing, and the after-taste, yum yum!

MOOSE. No, Dave!

DAVE. No, Paul? What could it be?

(**MOOSE** *comes up with GIANT JOINT.*)

A joint! Boy howdy!

MOOSE. Nothing stops those synapses snapping like killing off a couple thousand brain cells!

DAVE. But wait! If you act now, act psychotic!

(**DAVE** *pops up with a medicine bottle spewing PILLS.*)

MOOSE. Pills!

DAVE. Don't forget to get your Z's!

JAMIE. Stop there, Jo!

MOOSE. Stop there, Dave! There's no sense crapping, coughing & popping, if you can't throw up too!

(**MOOSE**: *big BOTTLE OF SCOTCH. THEY act drunk.*)

DAVE. Nothing gets you sicker…

BOTH. Than a big ol' quart of liquor!

MOOSE. Hey, that's no dry heaves!

JAMIE. Okay.

DAVE. Hold on, Paul! There's a late development in the game!

(*THEY pause, look at* **JAMIE.**)

JAMIE. So I had a few nips.

MOOSE. Nipping, puffing, popping & puking!

DAVE. What would the game be without it, Paul?

JAMIE. I wouldn't if you'd leave me alone.

MOOSE. Oh! Offense as defense, Dave, a beautiful move!

JAMIE. Please make them go away.

JO. What will you give me?

JAMIE. Uh! God! What do you want?

> (**JO** *smiles.* **PUPPETS** *fade.*)

JO. Got a nickel?

JAMIE. What?

JO. "You always have a nickel…"

JAMIE. *(Smiling)* Oh man. I can't believe you remember these things.

JO. *(In voice)* "You always have a nickel…"

BOTH. "…If you imagine that you do."

JAMIE. How do you even come up with that? I haven't thought of that in years.

> (**JO** *holds out cupped hands.*)

JO. Pick a nickel.

JAMIE. If I do, will you let me go to bed?

> (**PUPPETS** *pop up.*)

DAVE. Oo, deal making on the field, Paul! I'm not sure that's allowed!

JAMIE. Okay, okay.

> (**PUPPETS** *disappear.* **JAMIE** *reaches for a nickel.*)

JO. Just one.

JAMIE. "One is all you need."

> (*SHE picks an imaginary nickel out of* **JO's** *hands, holds it up, ready to flip it.*)

JO. You call.

JAMIE. Heads it's… "Good Vibrations"!

JO. Tails it's… "Wipeout"!

JAMIE. *(Stopping)* Not "Wipeout".

JO. Why?

JAMIE. I played it at the hospital.

JO. Really?

(**JAMIE** *nods.*)

I didn't know that.

JAMIE. Pick another.

JO. Well did –

JAMIE. Come on come on, pick something else.

JO. Ooookay, ladies & gentlemen, tails it's… "To Sir With Love"!

JAMIE. *(Disapproving.)* Oh!

JO. My pick! Poo-poo head.

JAMIE. *You* poo-poo head.

(**JAMIE** *flips the imaginary coin. As soon as SHE uncovers it,* **JO** *shouts.*)

JO. "To Sir With Love"!

JAMIE. No it's not!

JO. Yes it is, look at it!

JAMIE. I flipped it!

JO. I called it! Now put it in!

JAMIE. You don't –

JO. Put it in, let's go! E-2. "To Sir With Love" is E-2.

(THEY come together at an imaginary JUKEBOX.)

JAMIE. We never had an E-2.

JO. *My* jukebox.

JAMIE. It is not *your* jukebox!

JO. Stop stalling.

(**JAMIE** *protects the nickel.*)

JAMIE. It was always our jukebox! Now say it.

JO. Oh man, major poo-poo head.

(**PUPPETS** *up.*)

DAVE. It's a poo-poo head move, Paul!

MOOSE. That's right, Dave! Holding the nickel hostage, a cheap trick for total losers!

JAMIE. Say it.

MOOSE. Very well, it's *their* jukebox, Dave.

DAVE. Right, Paul, 'team spirit.'

JAMIE. Okay.

*(**PUPPETS** disappear. **JAMIE** drops the NICKEL in an imaginary slot. We hear it drop.)*

JO. E-2.

*(**JAMIE** pushes invisible SELECTION BUTTONS. Mechanisms come to life, clicking & whirring. A RECORD DROPS. NEEDLE hits record, scratchy & old: "To Sir With Love."*

*LIGHTS SHIFT to go-go super-stars as THEY take their places. **JO** launches into lip-synch & dance. The choreography is effortless, executed with the familiarity of hours of childhood repetition. THEY eventually lose themselves in it, laughing & hamming it up...)*

"The time has come
For closing books
And long last looks must end!"

*(Hands **JAMIE** imaginary mic.)*

JAMIE. "And as I leave
I know that I am
Leaving my best friend."

BOTH. "A friend who taught me right from wrong
And weak from strong,
That's a lot to learn.
What can I give you in return? ...
If you wanted the moon
I would try to make a start
But I
Would rather you let me give my heart.
To Sir, with love."

*(As the SONG ENDS and the LIGHTS shift back, **JAMIE***

suddenly grabs JO *in her arms, holds her tight.)*

JAMIE. Hold me, Jo.

JO. Okay.

JAMIE. The song made me sad.

(JO *holds her, hums gently.)*

JO. *(Sings softly)* "And as I go I know that I am leaving my best friend… "

JAMIE. I don't want you to ever leave me.

JO. Well, you're doing a good job.

(Insect voice.)

"She's squeezing the life out of me!"

JAMIE. *(Laughing)* Who's that?

JO. Caterpillar in my pocket.

JAMIE. Oh, okay then.

(JAMIE *looses her embrace.)*

I have fun with you. Even in the middle of the night when you wake me up & I'm crabby, you can still make me feel better than anyone else. Like a person again. And I just… don't feel it that much these days. You help me get above it. Which is amazing, since you're a total poo-poo head.

(JO *ruffles her hair,* THEY *push each other playfully.)*

JO. You crazy poo-poo head.

JAMIE. *You* crazy.

JO. Who put the glue in mom's shoes?

(THEY laugh.)

JAMIE. Who thought it up?

JO. Who actually did it?

JAMIE. Who stapled dad's shirt sleeves closed?

JO. Who ran away from home and took his charge card?

JAMIE. Who put peanut butter on the roof of the dog's mouth?

(THEY imitate a dog trying to lick the roof of it's mouth, laughing.)

Oh man, that was funny!

JO. Who did Nickel in a Jukebox?

JAMIE. Yeah, but I owed it to you, I got you in trouble with that whole 'odd man' thing.

JO. But you could always cheer me up.

JAMIE. Yeah, I could.

JO. That's why you played it?

JAMIE. What?

JO. "Wipeout." At the hospital.

*(**JAMIE** finds the SCOTCH BOTTLE on the bed.)*

JAMIE. Hey, look, your friends left the bottle!

JO. You left the bottle.

JAMIE. Did I?

JO. Did you dance?

JAMIE. When?

JO. At the hospital.

JAMIE. *(Searching)* Where's the crackers? See, you gave me an appetite.

JO. At the hospital.

JAMIE. Yeah.

(Opens the bottle, fills the cap.)

Cheers.

(Shoots it back, looks around.)

Did they leave that giant joint too?

JO. Did you sing?

JAMIE. Don't bring me down, okay? You got me feeling good, I thought that was the point.

JO. Is that the point?

*(**JO** holds out her hands.)*

Wanna nickel?

JAMIE. No.

(Pouring another capful.)

Want another drink? Yes.

(She drinks)

Ah. Yes I sang, I thought it would cheer you up.

JO. The whole thing, choreography too?

JAMIE. Not at first. You were in a coma. What could you see?

JO. Coma with my eyes closed?

JAMIE. Coma with your eyes half open, glazed. But then I did.

JO. You did?! The whole act?

JAMIE. I thought you might respond.

(**JAMIE** *pours another shot.*)

JO. I don't remember. Did I respond?

JAMIE. *(Offering glass to puppets)* Would they like some?

JO. They're smokin' dope. Come on, tell me.

JAMIE. I sang and danced around the room. Well *limped* around the room, I had this cast on my ankle and this crutch. And the nurse came in and turned the tape off and told me to stop it, it was making the numbers on your blood pressure thing go up. That's all, period, no more.

JO. *You* brought it up.

JAMIE. Well fuck me.

(**JAMIE** *drinks.*)

JO. Did you stop?

JAMIE. Yes, yes! Okay? And when her back was turned I flipped her off.

JO. Really?

JAMIE. Yes, in your behalf. And then I whispered to you fuck her, as soon as she was off shift I would come back and finish. – Can you get your friends back here, I wanna ask 'em something.

JO. They're asleep.

JAMIE. What?

JO. Let 'em sleep.

JAMIE. No! They can't sleep. *I* can't! You certainly can't!

JO. I am tired, Jamie.

JAMIE. No! No, you certainly are not!

> (**JAMIE***'s turn to bug Jo.*)

> You're the energetic one, the crazy character of the family! I was the wimp.

JO. You lived.

JAMIE. Oh, hah! You call this living?! Aach! This is not living! This is one long Yoo-Hoo moment! Yoo-Hoo!

> (*SHE looks for Yoo-Hoo under the bed, finds none.*)

> This is my twilight serenade!

> (*Holds out her hands to* **JO**.)

> Pick a nickel!

JO. How long can you –

JAMIE. Pick! Pick pick pick pick pick!

> (**JO** *picks one, prepares to flip it.*)

> Heads it's… "Wild Thing"!

JO. Tails it's "Wipeout."

> (*THEY look at one another.*)

JAMIE. Pick something else.

JO. I'll name it again tomorrow.

JAMIE. You're a damn brat.

JO. You wanted me here.

JAMIE. Not like this.

JO. Package deal, good with the bad, what're you gonna do?

JAMIE. I've been thinking of jumping out the window.

> (**JO** *&* **JAMIE** *stare, nickel held between them.*
>
> *A loud BUZZER sounds, UPSET CROWDS, SOME BOOING.* **PUPPETS** *up.*)

MOOSE. Oh! That's a bad call, Dave!

DAVE. Yes, Paul, the crowds are pretty unhappy! A forfeit would certainly cast a bad light on the game!

MOOSE. Cosmically speaking of course.

DAVE. Oh yes, cosmically speaking, big, big penalties!

MOOSE. Nothing troubles the season ticket holder more than an unfinished game!

DAVE. Unresolved, Paul!

MOOSE. Leaves the players with that uncomfortable sticky feeling! Options, Dave?

DAVE. Punt, Paul!

JAMIE. Punt?

MOOSE. Or bunting! Some of our greatest players have been bunters!

DAVE. Or a good, fleet runner up the middle!

MOOSE. Ace in the hole!

DAVE. Seven love, all the bases loaded!

MOOSE. Pay or play, Dave!

DAVE. Pay or play!

JO. You only live on the fourth floor. What do you think that's gonna do to you?

DAVE. Wow, that's a tough call, Paul!

MOOSE. No one likes to see an athlete get hurt!

JAMIE. Nothing near so bad as happened to you.

JO. I didn't feel it.

JAMIE. That's not how you looked under the car.

JO. I meant later.

JAMIE. You didn't see yourself!

JO. Actually I did.

JAMIE. I don't wanna talk about it!

JO. Okay.

(**JO** *lifts the nickel.*)

JAMIE. Don't, Jo.

JO. It's our last nickel.

(SOUND of NICKEL dropping in slot.)

JAMIE. No!

(JAMIE lunges to stop her, but JO clicks the jukebox BUT-TONS. LIGHTS FLICKER as the juke-box shifts & whirs.)

I swear, I'll cut my wrists!

(JAMIE digs madly in the night-stand, the NEEDLE drops onto scratchy record.)

I have a knife!

(Opening drum of "Wipeout".)

DON'T!

(SIMULTANEOUSLY: The LIGHTS FLICKER to an odd skew and JO drops on the bed, a RESPIRA-TOR MASK covering her mouth & nose. 'WIPEOUT' plays…

MOOSE, DAVE, and two creepy NURSE PUPPETS emerge, ALL in surgical masks. THEY move over JO's seizuring body in a bizarre dance. Slowly THEY close in over her, the VOICES OF DOCTORS & NURSES working despe-rately, dim sounds of MEDICAL MACHINES beeping. JAMIE tries to hide her head.)*

MOOSE. Do we have a pulse?

NURSE 1. No pulse.

DAVE. She's crashing.

JAMIE. Please stop…

MOOSE. Give me a heartbeat!

NURSE 2. We have code red.

DAVE. What the hell happened, she was stable!

JAMIE. Stop it, this is gross!

MOOSE. Somebody give me a count!

NURSE 1. Five minutes.

MOOSE. She's not responding!

JAMIE. Please stop it!

NURSE 2. What do you want to do?

DAVE. We could open her up.

MOOSE. Is there any next of kin?

NURSE 1. There's a sister.

NURSE 2. You want to call it?

DAVE. Where's the pump?

NURSE 1. What?

MOOSE. There's no air coming through!

NURSE 2. Code red.

DAVE. Is this off?!

NURSE 2. We have code red!

MOOSE. Oh my God, who stopped the respirator!

NURSE 2. Code red!

DAVE. Jesus Christ, who cut the –

(*JAMIE rises up, a severed RESPIRATOR TUBE in her hand.*)

JAMIE. ME! ME! I DID IT, OKAY? I'M NOT SORRY AND WE ALL KNOW IT!

(*The MUSIC cuts.*)

I'm not sorry, so why don't we just cut the crap!

(*The **PUPPETS** disappear, LIGHTS back to the single bedside lamp. JO's body remains lifeless on the bed.*)

I cut your respirator and you'd have done the same for me, if you'd seen yourself, with your face all bloated and your brain coming out the back of your head. Which didn't even happen 'til they tried to lift the car off you and dropped it.

(*JAMIE pulls the RESPIRATOR MASK off JO's face, gently pushes her eyes closed.*)

My sister Jo, irreversibly, irrevocably brain dead. When they said you were in a vegetative state, I just wanted you to jump up and say, "What, Pennsylvania parsnips?" P-word. Plosives are funny.

(SHE strokes JO'S *forehead.)*

There wasn't a goddamn doubt in me, the last thing you'd want was to lie there with empty eyes and have mom & dad watch you shrivel up. Jesus! It was scary, but it wasn't that hard. All I had to do was picture you pinned under the car, and cut it. And you know what? You'll like this, you know what I cut it with, Jo?

(SHE tries to rouse JO, *takes her in her arms & tries to show her.)*

Jo, look! Uncle Jack's old hunting knife, that he gave you when you were five, remember? Because you were sad 'cause they suspended you from kindergarten for insisting that men were odd!

*(*JAMIE *shakes her. No response.)*

Why the hell did you go & tell that to the teacher? That's such a stupid thing to suspend a little kid for. We just didn't know how to pray! ... Jo!

*(*JO *remains dead.)*

It was only a short thread. When that was the only thing holding you from freedom, it didn't seem like much. I thought it would cut you loose. I just didn't know... it was the only thing holding me to the world.

(SHE sinks down by the bed, still clutching the cut RES-PIRATOR TUBE.)

The planet Jupiter is 40 million miles away. If you sent someone from earth they wouldn't even arrive until 2,038. And for them to get back, it would take until they were 90 years old. If they ever got back at all. It's a lonely place, Jo. I just couldn't go there alone.

JO. You been on a high lonesome.

JAMIE. I don't think I can do it anymore.

*(*JO *sits up.)*

JO. Eyesight failin' and ink near out.

JAMIE. I've kept you a long time.

JO. "Forgive me, Janey..."

JAMIE. ...and consider I was lonesome.

(JO *kisses her head.*)

JO. I know. C'mere. ...

(*THEY sit together.* JO *touches the TUBE in Jamie's hand.*)

Think maybe ya carried that around long enough?

JAMIE. What'll happen if I let go?

JO. I'll stay with you 'til you fall asleep.

JAMIE. And then what?

JO. And then you get up, and have one hell of a bleary work day tomorrow.

JAMIE. And then?

JO. You come home, and eat a whole dinner, and go to sleep.

JAMIE. Alone?

(JO *nods.*)

Will *you* sleep?

JO. Yes. I'll be sleeping.

(JAMIE *surrenders the section of TUBE to* JO.

SHE goes to the bed and gets in. JO *comes and tucks her in.*

And then steps back.)

JAMIE. I'll dream of you.

JO. All the way home.

(JO *reaches for the light.*)

JAMIE. Jo?

JO. Hm?

JAMIE. Amen, Jo.

(JO *smiles.*)

JO. Odd man.

(*SHE snaps out the light.*

BLACKOUT. MUSIC: "To Sir With Love.")

PROP LIST

5 Puppets
   Paul the Moose - Puppet with movable mouth
   Tim the Pig - Puppet who's just stupid.
   Dave the Bird - Puppet with movable arms.
   2 Creepy Nurses - Creepy.
Surgical masks for 4 puppets
1 Trombone
Box of crackers
3 Bottles of Yoo-Hoo Chocolate drink
Confetti
1 Cigarette and Lighter
1 Alarm clock
1 Carton of cigarettes
1 Giant marijuana joint
1 Large bottle of pills
1 Bottle of scotch
Oxygen mask
Respiratory tube

OFF-OFF-BROADWAY FESTIVAL PLAYS

TWELFTH SERIES
The Brannock Device   The Prettiest Girl in Lafayette County   Slivovitz
Two and Twenty

THIRTEENTH SERIES
Beached   A Grave Encounter   No Problem   Reservations for Two
Strawberry Preserves   What's a Girl to Do

FOURTEENTH SERIES
A Blind Date with Mary   Bums   Civilization and Its Malcontents   Do Over
Tradition 1A

FIFTEENTH SERIES
The Adventures of Captain Neato-Man   A Chance Meeting Chateau Rene
Does This Woman Have a Name?   For Anne   The Heartbreak Tour
The Pledge

SIXTEENTH SERIES
As Angels Watch   Autumn Leaves   Goods   King of the Pekinese Yellowtail
Uranium   Way Deep   The Whole Truth   The Winning Number

SEVENTEENTH SERIES
Correct Address   Cowboys, Indians and Waitresses   Homebound   The Road
to Nineveh   Your Life Is a Feature Film

EIGHTEENTH SERIES
How Many to Tango?   Just Thinking   Last Exit Before Toll   Pasquini the
Magnificent   Peace in Our Time   The Power and the Glory
Something Rotten in Denmark   Visiting Oliver

NINETEENTH SERIES
Awkward Silence   Cherry Blend with Vanilla   Family Names   Highwire
Nothing in Common   Pizza: A Love Story   The Spelling Bee

TWENTIETH SERIES
Pavane   The Art of Dating   Snow Stars   Life Comes to the Old Maid   The
Appointment   A Winter Reunion

TWENTY-FIRST SERIES
Whoppers   Dolorosa Sanchez   At Land's End   In with Alma
With or Without You   Murmurs   Ballycastle

SAMUELFRENCH.COM

OFF-OFF-BROADWAY
FESTIVAL PLAYS

TWENTY-SECOND SERIES
Brothers   This Is How It Is   Because I Wanted to Say Tremulous   The Last
Dance   For Tiger Lilies Out of Season   The Most Perfect Day

TWENTY-THIRD SERIES
The Way to Miami   Harriet Tubman Visits a Therapist   Meridan, Mississippi
Studio Portrait   It's Okay, Honey   Francis Brick Needs No Introduction

TWENTY-FOURTH SERIES
The Last Cigarette   Flight of Fancy   Physical Therapy   Nothing in the World Like It
The Price You Pay   Pearls Ophelia   A Significant Betrayal

TWENTY-FIFTH SERIES
Strawberry Fields   Sin Inch Adjustable   Evening Education   Hot Rot
A Pink Cadillac Nightmare   East of the Sun and West of the Moon

TWENTY-SIXTH SERIES
Tickets, Please!   Someplace Warm   The Test   A Closer Look
A Peace Replaced   Three Tables

TWENTY-SEVENTH SERIES
Born to Be Blue   The Parrot   Flights   A Doctor's Visit
Three Questions   The Devil's Parole

TWENTY-EIGHTH SERIES
Along for the Ride   A Low-Lying Fog   Blueberry Waltz   The Ferry
Leaving Tangier   Quick & Dirty (A Subway Fantasy)

TWENTY-NINTH SERIES
All in Little Pieces   The Casseroles of Far Rockaway   Feet of Clay
The King and the Condemned   My Wife's Coat   The Theodore Roosevelt Rotunda

THIRTIETH SERIES
Defacing Michael Jackson   The Ex   Kerry and Angie   Outside the Box
Picture Perfect   The Sweet Room

THIRTY-FIRST SERIES
Le Supermarché   Libretto   Play #3   Sick   Pischer   Relationtrip

THIRTY-SECOND SERIES
Opening   Circuit Breakers   Bright. Apple. Crush
The Roosevelt Cousins, Thoroughly Sauced   Every Man   The Good Book

SAMUELFRENCH.COM

Printed in the United States
213249BV00005B/2/P